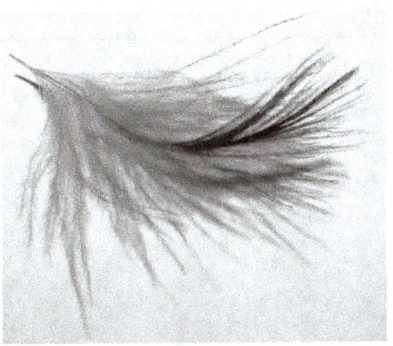

"A beautifully written story about
loss and second chances." — *Kirkus Reviews*

"…Dee is bottomless in her complexity, a woman
coping with her mother, mortality, and a bird in the
house… She's a protagonist worthy of the
reader's gripping interest."— *Kirkus Reviews*

Also by
Lynn Arbor

Intentional, A Novel

A Bird in the House

A novel

Lynn Arbor

A Bird in the House

Cover design by Lynn Arbor

ISBN 978-0-9862206-3-0

Library of Congress Control Number:
2017912518

Spring Forward Publishing

First Edition printed in USA

Contents

For John Bogner

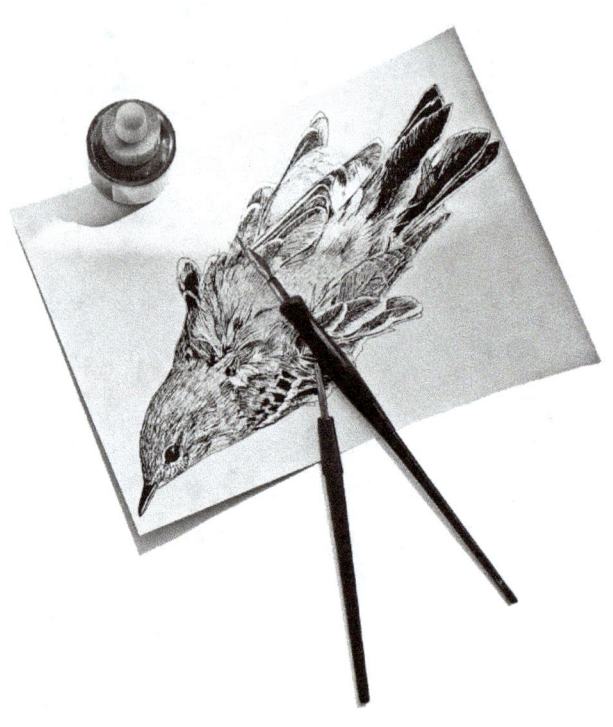

1. TWO WOMEN

"The caged bird dreams of clouds."
Japanese Proverb

Two women—one old, one ancient—sat on plastic chairs on their front porch. Chips of white paint fell from the porch rails and posts. A chunk of crumbling concrete had dropped away from a corner of the porch top, age softening the sharp edge into a curve, just as the women themselves crumbled before their own eyes, surfaces sagging and frameworks calcifying.

Dee Ellison Chope, the old woman, was the daughter of Bessie Burns Ellison, the ancient one. Bessie had already forgotten about the bird in the house. Dee still had most of her marbles, and however much she wanted to, she couldn't blank out the image of the dead bird she'd discovered in the fireplace that morning. A bird in the house is bad luck. Someone's gonna die. Superstitious? Yes. But her thoughts were on a roll—someone would die. Obviously. Eventually. They were both, after all, old.

The best way to go, Dee thought, would be pain-free, wearing clean underwear. If she got to pick, she'd prefer to die in her sleep, but then she'd be wearing no underwear and the big Detroit Red Wings t-shirt her son had sent her last Christmas. Dee wasn't a hockey fan, but it was a good shade of red, and if she were going to root, she'd root for the home team.

If she did go first, she'd be guilt-free—she wouldn't be responsible anymore. Not that she was in a hurry, she was content to go on living for quite a while, but after finding the bird in the fireplace, all those damn death thoughts had filled her head.

But, most important, if she died first who would take care of Bessie? Dee's daughter Amy had a husband, three kids, and a vineyard in Wisconsin to care for. Dee's son Paul was in Afghanistan, hopefully not getting shot by Osama bin Laden. And how about her only sibling, Georgie? He was just a few miles away, but she didn't trust him to take care of a toad. No, it was really better if she outlived Bessie.

Dee pulled a half-smoked cigarette from the pack in her sweater pocket (either making no connection, or ignoring the connection to life expectancy) and lit it. She closed her eyes and inhaled slowly. She'd never learned how to expel smoke in a ring, so she just turned her face away from her mother and exhaled a small cloud.

As the smoke left her lips, Dee closed her eyes and imagined floating high above the house. The sky held her lightly. It didn't speak or howl or rumble as the sky sometimes does. It was silent. The vast sky didn't ask when she'd fix its dinner, or what day it was, or how come Georgie never called. The sky was quiet and beautiful and blue.

It had been sixteen years since Dee nearly died in the car accident. Unable to walk back then, trapped in a hospital bed—she had visualized herself flying—flying out of the hospital room's window, out over the parking lot, then north as far and as high as she could go. After months of therapy she could walk again, but she couldn't fly—she could only fantasize, which she did often. Realistically, she understood that she'd never fly on her own, but there were options: maybe ziplining over some exotic jungle, or skydiving. Or how about hang gliding, which would probably be the quietest and closest to her fantasy?

She reached into the pocket of her sweater for her tiny nail scissors and cut off the burning tip of her cigarette. The burning end dropped into a flowerpot she'd filled with sand, and she watched the embers turn to soot. The rest of the cigarette went back into the pack. Cigarettes were expensive. As part of the weaning process, she allowed herself one each day, enjoyed at various stressed moments with a single deeply inhaled puff.

She knew exactly what was coming next, the tone of her mother's voice, every single word about to be spoken, but the smoke was worth it, if only for reasons of defiance.

Bessie, whose vision worked just fine, maybe too fine, said her usual, "Smoking can kill you, and if you want my opinion, Dee, it just doesn't look ladylike either."

Bessie had done her best to train Dee to be a proper woman. She had sent Dee to high school in a panty girdle, and she constantly reminded her not to frown, saying she'd regret every sad face she made when she got older.

"Just so's you know, Dee, you don't want to be cranky-looking later in life."

"Yes, Bessie," the obedient daughter would reply, but when Bessie left the room, Dee would contort her face into expressions that would be scary around a campfire with a flashlight shining up under her chin.

"And sit ladylike," Bessie would say, which meant ankles crossed and knees pressed together and pushed to one side, and don't forget hands should be folded on your lap.

"Yes, Bessie," teenage Dee would reply, and when her mother wasn't looking, she'd spread her knees wide like a man claiming space.

Bessie was also the grammar police, although her service revolver was loaded with blanks. Bessie, who had graduated from high school in 1936, insisted on her daughter using proper English. It's always, "You and I", never "you and me." Dee got corrected in front of her friends, but often the correction was incorrect. If Bessie overheard Dee say to a friend, "Kim can't come to the movies with you and me," she'd pop in with, "You and I, Dee. It's you and I." And "Ain't" was as bad as cursing. Low class. A civilized person should have standards, ya know.

Bessie reached out and turned her daughter's face toward her, then poked at Dee's cheek with her twisted arthritic index finger.

"And see, Dee, all these tiny red veins on your cheeks and these little wrinkles around your lips. That's what smoking gets you. Why are you doing that to yourself?"

This face poking was something new, something that wasn't part of Bessie's usual scold repertoire.

Dee said nothing.

"You're very wrinkly. How old are you anyway?" Bessie asked her daughter, not facetious or sarcastic, just wanting to know.

"Sixty-four. How old are you?"

"Not as old as you, that's for sure," her mother said.

"You were ninety last month."

"I was not. You're lyin', Dee." Then Bessie laughed, "That's a good one. Ninety." And she shook her head and laughed some more.

Dee was thinking that if Bessie died first she could smoke more without getting scolded, but that didn't appeal. What did appeal? If she was the last woman standing she wouldn't have anyone to take care of, so what would she do? Fly? Ride up high in a hot air balloon? Although the thought was tantalizing, it slipped away quickly, overcome by her sure knowledge that Bessie would outlast her.

Bessie went back to trailing the tip of her finger around Dee's face, peering at her so close up that Dee felt the heat of her mother's breath and smelled recently digested eggs.

"Your face looks like a child took a red pen and doodly-daddled all over your cheeks. You should go look in a mirror, Dee." Then Bessie sighed. Her eyes took on that dreamy look she got when remembering ancient history.

"Dee, do you remember that nice pen set I got Georgie? It had all those little nips that he stuck into the end of the wooden holder. Some nips made fat lines and some made a fine thin line just like here on your face. Of course, since these lines on your face are red, it would'a had to a been red ink, not black."

"Nibs, Bessie. Nibs, not nips," Dee said.

Bessie didn't remember that Dee was her daughter, but she remembered an incident that happened fifty years ago. Dee was impressed that the trapdoor of her mother's memory had let out that much information, except that it was mostly wrong.

The crow quill pen set had been Dee's, a gift from her father, who had high hopes that she'd be an artist one day. Georgie, her younger brother, her mother's little prince, had wanted it. And guess what? Screaming, thrashing about, whining, begging, and pleading works. Give him what he wants and he'll shut up.

Georgie won that round, but it wasn't enough. Smug, with the devil in his eyes, her ten-year old brother put a sharp tiny nib into the wooden penholder, dipped it into the bottle of permanent black India ink, and with a fast fury stabbed Dee's bare arm. She got a tattoo, a cluster of black dots, faded after all these decades, but still evidence that her younger brother had scarred her for life.

You'd think that stabbing his sister with *her* gift would result in one of the following:

a). Georgie getting spanked,

b). Georgie getting sent to his room,

c). The pen set going back to its rightful owner.

You'd think.

After Prince George tattooed Dee, he started to cry. Teary-eyed he apologized to his parents, but not to his fourteen-year-old sister. He sweet-talked his parents into remembering how adorable he was. Precious boy. Check out those dimples.

How funny that Bessie remembered the whole incident so differently. Whose memory was right? Dee's probably. Besides, Dee had the tattoo to prove it. She pushed up her sleeve, double-checking her own memory.

Yes. The once tight cluster of black dots was there, but after more than fifty years and with the expansion of the skin on her arm, each dot drifted further from the others.

Dee pulled her sleeve back down. It was a bit cool out, but still so nice being outside after the confinement of winter. Although the temperature was in the mid-sixties, she had helped her mother into a light cotton turtleneck, a sweater and a fleece jacket. Bessie seemed to get colder with each passing year. Eventually, all the heat would leave her. Dee patted Bessie's hand, not sure why she felt the need, maybe just checking Bessie's temperature.

A small breeze ruffled the newborn chartreuse leaves on the big oaks and fluffed the feathers of the first robin she'd seen this year.

April 22, 2008.

How could it be? Her life was flying by. *Slow down,* she wanted to say to time. *Make a nest. Lay some eggs.* It was an afternoon too beautiful to be thinking about aging and death and being on the down side of life's hill.

She stood, stretched out her back, and went down the front steps. A bright green weed had shot up through the middle of the prickly blue juniper beside the porch. She tugged at it. She tugged again.

"Pokeweed," Bessie sang out from the porch.

"Pokeweed? Really? That sounds like something that would grow in Georgia or Mississippi. Not in Michigan."

"Grows all over, I guess," Bessie said. "Ya know poor people eat pokeweed. They pick it young and cook it, or maybe I'm thinkin' of them eating dandelions or something else, I forget things sometimes. But just so's you know, I do remember that it's poisonous. I'm not sure if it's the berries or the leaves or maybe the roots, but something's poisonous."

Bessie couldn't remember how old she was, but she remembered plants. Plants were firmly planted inside Bessie's brain.

Dee let go of the weed. Maybe she should wear gloves to pull it.

"Anyways, Dee, you're gonna need a shovel to get that outta there," Bessie said. "They have big roots, even small ones like that. In the summer it'll get berries. The birds love those berries. If you let it grow that purple stem will get as thick as a hot dog. I love hot dogs, Dee."

Dee was tired or maybe just weary, without the energy to walk around the house to get the shovel from the garage. Later. She'd do it later, like so many things that she didn't do, she'd do it later. How often did she feel so worn out? Like all the juice, all the joy was sucked right out of her? Later she'd get the shovel and dig the weed. Later she'd bury the bird, but for now the bird was still dead in the fireplace. It wasn't going to be flying off anywhere, and neither was she.

When Bessie was younger, the yard had been beautiful, lush with flowers and neatly pruned shrubs. Bessie was visual, she liked things to be pretty and she loved gardening. Bessie herself had been a beauty, a head turner.

Dee remembered how her beautiful young mother would sit on the lavender cushioned stool in front of her vanity turning this way and that, admiring her own baby blue eyes, her sweet perky nose, her high cheekbones, her delicate jawline, her equine neck. Vanity. Did the name for the mirrored dresser come first, or the vain behavior?

Bessie's vanity had hurt Dee before she could even talk. When other mothers were repeating to their babies, "Say, Mama. Can you say Mama for me," repeating over and over while Dada was away at work, trying to get the first word out of their baby's mouth to be Mama, not Dada, no, or cookie, Dee's mother was teaching her tiny daughter to call her Bessie. Was it some strange post-partum depression that made her not want to be seen as Dee's mother?

No, more likely, it was vanity.

"Mirror, mirror on the wall," Dee had imagined her mother saying as she admired herself. But Bessie's mirror was mute. Her answer was visual—Bessie *was* the fairest of them all. Even strangers in the grocery store mattered, and when they saw Bessie, when they turned and stared, gawked even, wondering if that gorgeous woman was some movie star, they should imagine that the tiny girl in the buggy or tagging behind her was some orphan or waif that this lovely woman had taken into her magnanimous care. This homely child couldn't possibly have burst forth from between the silken thighs of the beautiful one.

Then when Dee was four, Georgie, the beautiful son was born. Bessie's heart was swollen big with love and generosity. When her new son was learning to speak, Bessie trained him: *Georgie, say Mama, say Mama, Georgie.* Learning by rote, over and over: *say Mama, say Mama.* To encourage her son to call her Mama, Bessie invited Dee to start calling her Mama too, but it was too late. Dee refused, and, in fact, never in her life called Bessie "Mother".

Dee tramped a few feet out into the green and yellow carpet that was their lawn. Dandelions. Dozens of dandelions. The warm air invited those obstinate yellow blooms to shout out their arrival en masse. The neighbors, with their perfectly manicured lawns, must be pooping their pants. She was surprised that no one had called the city and reported them. The neighbors tolerated them. No one ever offered to help the two old women, but then she really didn't expect them to—people had their own lives and lawns to deal with. Maybe as they drove down their pleasant block, they closed one eye as they passed the Ellison house. Maybe they pretended that Bessie and Dee didn't exist. Or maybe they were just polite, not wanting to impose their yard preferences on the old ladies.

When she thought about what the neighbors might think of her, she wanted to be hostile toward them, but she didn't blame them. They worked hard—probably. They worked hard at whatever they did and hired lawn services to come mow and edge and fertilize. She couldn't afford to hire someone.

It embarrassed her at the core of her being that this house, this lawn, this eyesore, didn't reflect who she was. If she had the energy, she'd go door to door and apologize for being a bad neighbor. But if she had that much energy, shouldn't she use it to tidy up their yard?

There was an old push mower in the garage and maybe she'd get it out and push it. Maybe she'd get up some steam and mow the lawn, although the last time she tried the old mower just bent the grass. It needed sharpening, just like the women in the house. She could load the mower and her mother into her car and go get them all sharpened. That thought made her smile, but then she frowned wondering how she'd get the mower into her little car. Nothing was ever easy.

One other lawn on their block of large old houses (Tudors, Victorians, cape cods, bungalows, craftsmen and colonials) could stand a pedicure, which helped Dee relax about the imperfections of their own yard. She bent down and picked a yellow dandelion flower, then another, then another, gathering them into a bouquet. If she picked them before the flowers turned to puffs of seed, maybe she could stop them from spreading to the neighbors.

As she headed back up the porch stairs, the bones and cartilage in her left kneecap and ankle creaked. Mowing would be painful. The ground was uneven, dipping here and there, hard on a damaged body. Walking carefully, avoiding pitfalls as she picked the yellow blooms wasn't so wrenching on her left side as chugging along behind the mower would be. What she needed was a good lube job, plus a sharpening and oiling. She laughed out loud.

"What's funny?" Bessie asked.

"I picked you flowers. Smell," Dee said, and as she sat back down on her chair, she held out the dandelions to her mother. Bessie put the bouquet against her nose and sniffed, snorting in dandelion pollen and then sneezing so hard she blew some of the dandelion petals off their heads. They both laughed.

"That was funny," Bessie said.

Then her eyes widened as a freckle of memory came back, and she chuckled. "Just so's you know, Dee. I know what else is funny," she said, wagging her index finger at Dee. "Dandelions smell like weeds."

She shook the dandelions under her daughter's nose. "I just gave you a dandelion kiss."

They sat there laughing for a time, and then Bessie said, "So when're we having some lunch? That pokeweed got me thinking about hot dogs."

"We just had lunch. Remember, Bessie? I made you a fried egg sandwich with cheese. Remember? Just an hour ago, remember?"

Bessie looked huffy. "No, we couldn't a had lunch, cause I'm hungry. I think we didn't have any breakfast either. I think you're trying to starve me, Dee. That's what I think."

"But, don't you remember, Bessie. We sat at the kitchen table and I read the Detroit Free Press to you. The weather. Going up to the 70's today, but then cold again tomorrow. We even had some potato chips. You said it was all delicious."

"Nope." Bessie shook her head adamantly. "You're just making that up. You're wantin' me to starve to death."

"Put your hand up in front of your mouth and blow. You have egg breath."

"My smeller doesn't work that good anymore and you know it, Dee. You're just trying to trick me into thinkin' I ate."

Dee got up from her porch chair and went into the house, the day was just starting and she was already exhausted. Pokeweed was poisonous. She could cook some up with a little sautéed bacon and onion, but whom would she feed it too? If she ate it herself who would take care of Bessie? If she fed it to Bessie...

She put the pokeweed out of her mind.

2. A BIRD IN THE HOUSE

"A bird in the hand is worth two in the bush."
English / Irish / Italian Proverb

At the kitchen sink Dee splashed water on her face, hoping the water would work like an energy potion. In her mind she created a TV commercial for this miracle product—water. She imagined the packaging, pale blue like sky. H_2O The Invigorator. But the H_2O face splash did little for her energy level, so she let the product campaign go, and stood for a second listening to NPR— something about voter turnout in the Pennsylvania primary election.

She took the vintage radioactive red Fiestaware cup from the cupboard, filled it with hot coffee, added cream and sugar, and took it out to her mother.

Bessie reached up for the cup with both hands, and when it was firmly in her grasp, she said, "Oh, Dee, I was just thinkin' that I'd like a cup of coffee. Did ya know that this is my most favorite cup?"

"I did."

"Aren't you sweet."

Dee took a tissue from her pocket and gently wiped away little flecks of yellow dandelion dust from her mother's upper lip.

*

There was no getting around it—Dee was the one who would have to deal with the dead bird. She left Bessie on the front porch with her cup of coffee.

In the living room she knelt in front of the fireplace with her great-grandmother peering down at her from a gilded picture frame above the mantle. The dim room had a golden glow from the sun burning through the aged and brittle window shades. Bessie liked the shades drawn so the furniture (a hodgepodge of inherited Victorian armchairs, a classic Corbusier chaise, an Eames chair, and the oriental carpet) wouldn't fade. Lovely stuff. But fifty or sixty years of butts shifting and lifting, hands rubbing and fiddling wore black leather down to gray and brown leather down to beige; feet shuffling and stamping wore the rich colored oriental yarns in the rug down to a frayed and frazzled backing the color of paper grocery bags. A long forgotten and forgiven guest had dropped a drink—most likely a Tom Collins, a Singapore Sling, or some other alcoholic concoction chic in the fifties—taking a nibble off the edge of the coffee table's kidney-shaped plate glass top. The overstuffed sofa (the most comfortable seating in the room, if you avoided a certain spot where an obnoxious spring would goose you) sagged with exhaustion. Even wonderful things wear out.

The baby grand piano's ivories could have used some Crest whitening strips. Of course, there had been piano lessons from the time Dee was five until she was fifteen, you can't have a baby grand piano in your living room with your daughter middle C illiterate. The son never had piano obligations. The piano and Dee's car both got regular tune-ups—Dee liked playing and driving.

The glass doors of the fireplace had trapped the bird; she could see dusty smudges on the inside of the glass where it had banged itself trying to escape. The bird was a sparrow, perhaps a chimney sweep sparrow. Occasionally, she'd see hawks gliding high above their yard peering down, surveying the landscape, looking for movement, hunting for something: scampering chipmunks, pre-occupied squirrels, a neighbor's yapping Shih Tzu. Maybe a Santa hawk got it, and as a late Christmas gift dropped it down the chimney, like a cat would bring it's owner a dead mouse, a treasure, a present, *see what a good, smart, hunter kitty I am.* The hawks came from the Detroit Zoo several blocks away from their house. Once when she was a child, she thought she heard a lion in the night, but that was impossible, the lions were too far away to hear.

The zoo was nestled in the suburbs two miles north of Detroit. As a child, from her second story bedroom window she could see the zoo's water tower above the rooftops, white and rusty with big black letters. A few years ago the old water tower had been painted like a sunset—purple grading down to pale dusty pink with black silhouettes of wild animals and humans parading around the bottom—pretty for a water tower. Saplings planted in her youth had grown into giant oaks and maples, so now, when full-leafed summer arrived, the view of the water tower would be hidden in green, and in winter the water tower was blurred by a scramble of naked tree branches. Now it was beautiful (for a water tower) and she couldn't see it from her bedroom window. Was it a cruel irony that she'd only been able to see it easily when it was ugly?

Dee wore non-latex gloves bought at Costco—one of the two boxes of 200 gloves had already been used up. She put on a fresh pair when she cleaned chicken or her mother's bottom (sometimes Bessie needed help in that area).

Delicately, she lifted the bird from the fireplace floor and held it in her gloved hand. As she examined the perfect little feathers, tiny feet, and black dead eyes, she decided that the bird was female, not knowing if males in the sparrow family had brighter colors than the females. It was bad luck that she was in the house. Maybe the bad luck of the bird in the house was its own death and no one else would die. But still, it was innocent, probably just perched on the chimney, toppled over and fell in, trapped in the fireplace, trapped in the prison of this big old house.

Carefully, Dee got up from the floor, holding the bird in one gloved hand, while helping herself up with the other. On damp days or when she got into a difficult position, like this one, her left leg and particularly her left ankle gave her pain. If she ran her finger over her ankle where nerves had been severed, there was still an unpleasant tingly numbness, but she could walk and she was grateful for that.

Maybe there was an old shoebox that she could bury the bird in. It was too beautiful to just throw in the trash. This was a tiny bird, barely filling her gloved hand, and a shoebox would mean having to dig a big hole, so she decided to wrap the bird in a kitchen towel and bury it that way.

In the kitchen she laid the bird on a paper plate and sifted through a drawer until she found an old dishtowel worn so thin that it was almost transparent, but it was soft. Not that it would matter to the bird. It mattered to her. Once she'd had a life, had fluttered around in the treetops singing her little bird song. Once she'd been free.

A shout came from the front porch, "Dee! Dee, come quick!"

With the plate of bird in one hand and the towel in the other, she hurried out to Bessie. Her mother's face was a Greek tragedy.

Bessie had always diligently avoided frowns and scowls. Whenever she realized that they'd arrived on her face, she'd hurry to release them and make her expression neutral. The theory that you can read an old person's face for her history or past behavior wouldn't hold true in Bessie's case. She had carefully created a pleasant old woman's face by spending her lifetime controlling her expressions.

"Goodness, what's wrong?" She considered telling Bessie that such a frowny face would make wrinkles, but didn't.

"I need to know, promise me you'll tell me the truth, Dee. Promise me."

"About what?"

"Tell me if I did something bad. I must have done something awful, otherwise why wouldn't Georgie come see me or even call me. Do you think I might've hurt your brother's feelings?"

The old refrain. Bessie scared the crap out of her, and it was just the Georgie chorus.

"No, Bessie, you didn't do anything wrong. Georgie's just a jackass, that's all."

Bessie's face pinched into a scolding mask. "You shouldn't talk about your brother that way, and you shouldn't use such ugly words either. I raised you better than that kind of talk, Dee." Bessie's memory slipped in and out. Now she remembered that Dee was her daughter, a half hour before she had thought she was younger than Dee.

Suddenly, Bessie's face smoothed as she remembered to correct her expression, which followed by a straightening of the spine, posture mattered too. You can't scold your children while slouching. It just doesn't look right. Be firm. Get taller. Stretch up your spine.

The scolded daughter's shoulders sagged. She shook her head, but didn't respond.

"What's that on the plate, Dee? Did you bring me some lunch? A hot dog? A bologna sandwich, I hope." She clapped her hands like a happy six-year-old.

Dee lowered the paper plate so Bessie could see the dead bird.

"I can't eat that. It's not even cooked. Why would you feed me a raw bird? It still has feathers."

"It's not your lunch, Bessie. It's the sparrow that fell down the chimney."

Dee put the plate on the porch railing and carefully wrapped the bird in the towel.

"A bird in the house is bad luck, a bad omen, Dee. Did I ever tell you that? Do you remember the day before your father died when we found a dead bird on the kitchen floor? I wonder how it got in there anyway. Remember that?"

Dee didn't remember any dead bird on the kitchen floor—ever. Maybe Bessie was remembering something from her childhood. Who's, what's, where's, when's, and why's got misfiled in Bessie's memory storage system. She'd never get a job as a reporter.

"I'm going to bury it. Will you come around to the back yard with me, please?"

Before they started down the front porch steps, Dee put the towel-wrapped bird on the porch rail. It meant two trips up and down the stairs, but it was safer that way. Years ago, after the car accident, the neurologist had taught Dee—do one thing at a time.

"Okay, Bessie, be careful," Dee said, as they started down the concrete stairs. "Hold onto the rail and I'll hold your other hand."

When Bessie was standing steady on the sidewalk, Dee went back up the steps and got the bird on the paper plate, and then holding her mother's hand, they started a slow walk around the house.

"I should have my cane, Dee, don't you think? It's very valuable and we shouldn't just leave it up on the porch for any Tom, Dick or Harry to snatch."

Bessie stood still while Dee made a third trip up the six porch stairs. She returned with the straight black cane and handed it to her mother.

Bessie, who was surprisingly sure on her feet, held the cane up to Dee, and said, "See this top piece, Dee. See that. That's real gold. This was my father's cane. He had it made after he panned for gold in Colorado when he was a young man. This gold handle came from the actual gold he found. And that bottom bit there, that's iron or something strong. And you know what, Dee?"

She stopped then, stood still, waiting for Dee to ask *what*. So Dee complied, and said, "What?" even though she already knew *what*.

"This cane reminds me of my father. He was a good strong man, good as gold. Dee, if anything happens to me, you keep this cane. It's valuable. You keep it safe."

Dee had heard this before and just nodded.

"What's that in your hand?" Bessie asked.

"The bird. Remember, Bessie, the bird fell into the fireplace, and I'm going to bury her."

"A bird in the bush is worth two in the hand," Bessie said.

"I think it's the other way around."

There were two Crosley Griffith metal lawn chairs with their yellow metal faded almost white and a dilapidated old picnic table in the backyard. The chairs looked dusty and rusty, but still, it was a safe place for Bessie to sit, better than the picnic table bench that might collapse.

Dee got a trowel from the garage and then surveyed the yard—flowerbeds had turned to weed beds, and the vegetable garden had become a mini-jungle. Bessie had been the one with the green thumb in the family, but years ago the garden had become too much for her to maintain. On the east side of the yard, there was an area surrounded by cyclone fence, the dog run. Woofie's space, a good place to bury the bird. Woofie was long gone; she died old and arthritic when Dee was in junior high and they never got another dog.

She jiggled the rusty latch until the gate to the dog run opened. Tall weeds and junk trees had grown up in the space—no one had been in here in years. As she opened the gate and heard the creaking sound, a sick feeling came over her and with it a memory, she was in the dog run with Woofie. She remembered her mother bringing her out here and locking her in the dog run with the Husky. Bessie told her not to step in the doggie doodoo, then left her and went back into the house to take care of her precious new baby Georgie. She must have been four years old when she was left for hours in the dog run.

Long ago the neurologist had told her that when someone with a traumatic brain injury can't remember something they make up details to fill the blank spaces. Was she making this up? She could see it so clearly, and she remembered the feelings of abandonment and the thick fur where she buried her face. This was an old memory. The doctor told her that distant memories could be clearer and more accessible. She still couldn't remember the days right before the accident, and that was expected, but old memories should be real, shouldn't they?

She found a relatively clear spot where she dug a hole, and settled the bird into the grave. She whispered, "Sleep well," as she patted dirt over the sparrow in a small mound.

When she had finished her task, her mother was no longer on the chair. She felt a moment of panic, but then she saw Bessie standing in the weedy vegetable garden pointing with the cane.

"Asparagus," she called out. "I see asparagus. Get a knife, Dee."

Dee gave a "Don't move," order to Bessie and hurried inside for a paring knife. When she came back outside Bessie had left the weed garden and was back sitting on the chair with her back to the house, waving the cane in the air like a conductor at the Detroit Symphony Orchestra.

"I got tired," Bessie said. "What are you doing with that knife?"

"Asparagus. Remember, you found asparagus."

Then with a strange foreign accent, Bessie said, "She forgets sometimes."

Occasionally Bessie would admit her forgetfulness and do a little sing-song with a foreign accent. "Sometimes she forget," she'd say, impersonating a stranger with broken English, maybe a Russian immigrant, a foreign visitor explaining her failing memory, a voice other than her own telling a truth that the actual woman didn't want to face. Other times, there was simple denial. But then both were the same, and who could blame her?

"Me too. Sign we're getting old." Then standing in front of her mother, she asked, "Did you lock me in the dog run when Georgie was a baby?"

She watched Bessie's face, saw the guilty little pull back of her body and the sudden slouch in her shoulders, and knew, no matter what her mother said, that her own memory was true.

"Now, how should I remember something like that, that was years and years and years ago? I don't remember, and anyway, Dee, you loved that dog. You called that dog Mommy. Just so's you know, I think you did it to hurt me, Dee. That's what I think." There was an impatient, irritable tone in Bessie's voice.

Then she gave an abrupt *so there* nod of her head, and said, "You liked being with the dog."

"Jesus, Bessie. Damn," Dee whispered.

"I heard that, Dee. Stop swearing. Did I not raise you better than that?"

You didn't raise me, Bessie. I was raised by wolves, raised by Cain, raised by my own damn self, raised by a dog I called Mommy. You didn't raise me. She didn't remember calling Woofie Mommy.

Out loud, Dee said, "I was four."

"Remember how pretty Georgie was with all that blond hair, and those precious little dimples. You, on the other hand, were as bald as a melon and nearly totally chinless. You certainly didn't get your lack of chin from my side of the family." She stopped speaking for a moment, looked puzzled and said, "Maybe your lack of chin came from your father's side?"

Dee—choosing to ignore Bessie's comment— walked away then, back to the garden to look for the asparagus stalks. Bessie followed, swatting at weeds with the cane.

"I don't see any asparagus. There's just weeds," Dee said.

Bessie pointed the cane. "There, and there, and over there, shooting up through that tangle of creeping Charlie and creeping Jenny and purslane. See the ferns? Just so's you know, if you see the dried ferns and move them aside a bit, you'll see a few stalks. They're probably tough, but maybe they'd be good tasting."

Eagle eyes, like a hawk hovering, her mother saw several stalks of asparagus hiding in the weeds. Yes, there they were, but Dee was more impressed with Bessie's memory of creeping weed names. She'd forgotten that she'd had breakfast and lunch, but remembered creeping Charlie. The human brain was baffling.

"Someone should weed this garden," Bessie said.

"And who would that someone be?"

With a devilish grin Bessie wagged her bent arthritic index finger at Dee.

"No, no, Bessie," Dee said, and grinned back at her mother, and imitating, wagged her finger. "But, really, would you like to do a little weeding? I could bring the chair over here for you."

Bessie's eyebrows went up and she nodded like a small child offered ice cream, so Dee hurried for the chair before Bessie had time to forget what the plan was. Then she grabbed the trowel she'd been using to dig the bird's grave, and got Bessie settled-in clearing out the creeping weeds around the asparagus.

"I need a bucket from the garage for the weeds," Bessie said.

When Dee returned with the bucket, she shifted Bessie's pile of pulled weeds into the metal pail.

"Hand me that knife," Bessie said, all business, as if she were a surgeon asking for a scalpel, or as though there hadn't been a gap of years since she had worked in the garden. She cut the stalks, then handed Dee the asparagus dripping moisture from its cuts, and continued the weeding, her torso folded over her stomach with hot dogs and bologna sandwiches forgotten. Competent, Bessie seemed so happy, content, doing something that she had always loved. For a bit of time her mother wasn't a needy old woman. This was good for her, Dee decided. Maybe they could come out here every day when the weather was nice.

Five minutes later—like a little kid that you've dressed in a snowsuit, mittens, boots, gloves, and a hat with earflaps, and sent out to play in the snow—Bessie was tired, so they went in the house.

3. SUNDOWN

"Every bird flies with its own wings."
Swahili Proverb

Asparagus was something they hadn't had in years—too expensive for their budget. Meanwhile, out at the back of their yard this wonder of life had grown up and died back, and grown up again for years without their knowing it was there. What else in the world had they missed because they hadn't been looking?

Dinner was special—asparagus and fish (brain food) that Dee had gotten on sale. Instead of the usual dinner in front of the TV in the living room, they celebrated at the dining room table with cloth napkins and silverware set improperly. Dee had handed Bessie two knives, two forks and two spoons, and asked her to set the table. Bessie held them in her hand and just stared at them. Was she questioning what they were for, or just unsure of the sequence of cutlery beside a plate?

"Just give us each a knife, a fork and a spoon."

"I don't want to," Bessie said, and looked angry. "You do it."

"No, try. They don't have to be perfect."

So Bessie slammed the silverware down in the center of the table.

"Okay, then," Dee said. "Have a seat and I'll bring out our dinner." She left the silverware where it was, while she went in the kitchen and filled their plates.

When her dinner was in front of her, Bessie stared at her plate as though she didn't know what it was, then picked up an asparagus spear with her fingertips.

"Do I like this?" she asked, waving it in the air.

"Yes, you love it. It's your favorite vegetable, Bessie."

"Are you sure?"

"Try it."

Bessie put an end of the spear, uncut, into her mouth. Frowned. But after a moment she smiled.

"Yes, I like it."

The asparagus was perfect, not tough or stringy. It was amazing, Dee thought, that left untended for years it survived and survived well. And she wondered, are people as strong as asparagus. Hearty. Left untended can we stay moist and delicious? She was sure that Bessie couldn't survive without her. Her mother needed feeding and watering, ever since the weeds in her brain had been taking over. And compared to earlier in the day, Bessie seemed much weedier.

When the meal was finished, she got Bessie settled on the living room couch with the news on TV, while she went back to the kitchen to clean up. In a life filled with so many chores that she wasn't crazy about doing, dishwashing was a pleasure. Having her hands in the warm bubbles, holding them under the water and just taking some slow deep breaths relaxed her. Even wiping the stove and countertops gave her satisfaction. She took her time, and thought about the perfect meal: asparagus grilled in a pan with butter, the cod poached in a little milk, new potatoes with some sprinkled parsley. She was pleased with herself.

She dried her hands and went into the living room.

Bessie wasn't there.

She checked the bathroom. The door was open and no one was inside. She called her mother's name. She rushed upstairs and checked all the rooms—no Bessie. She went outside, then into the garage, then back to the garden. The sky was pink on the western horizon, grading up to purple like the colors on the Detroit Zoo water tower. Indigo was sliding across the sky.

She felt hysterical. How could she find her mother in the dark? She jabbed at herself for changing their routine. Dinner was special, and yet it made Bessie more unsettled than ever. Dee should have cut up the asparagus and the cod and the potatoes and layered them in a bowl like Bessie liked. She should have tucked a kitchen towel into the top of Bessie's shirt as usual. She should have brought Bessie her bowl of food in the living room with the TV blasting the latest news. She was flogging herself with should have's.

She stood panicky on the front sidewalk, then far down the block she saw a silhouette, and though not really sure it was Bessie, she hurried toward the distant figure, wishing she were able to run. As Dee got closer she recognized the posture, as straight as a model practicing her runway walk with a stack of books on her head. Bessie had perfect, regal posture, especially impressive considering her age.

As she got closer she heard her mother calling out, "Georgie, Georgie," with her hands cupped like a megaphone.

A woman was with her. Dee, panting and too winded to speak, nodded at the woman, smiled, but had to rest with one hand on her knee, while rubbing her left ankle with the other.

The woman asked, "Is Georgie her dog? What kind is it?"

Pit bull, Dee wanted to say, but immediately realized that a pit bull running loose in the neighborhood would scare the woman.

"Her son," she said.

The woman looked startled. "Oh," she said.

Then with a conspiratorial nod, she asked, "Can I help? I could drive you back home."

Dee thanked her and told her that the walk was good for them. As they walked home, Dee realized that a new wrinkle had been added to her life—Bessie wandered.

This meant that she could no longer let her mother out of her sight. She patted her sweater pocket, hoping for a cigarette. There wasn't one.

So this was going to be her life: tracking, trailing, feeding, washing, wiping and tending, until one day when she, Dee, fell asleep and never woke up. She'd never fly. Caregiver. She was the caregiver and it's pretty well known that care-getters often outlive their caregivers.

4. LUNCH

"Fat cats and thin birds can share a yard,
but thin cats and fat birds, no way."
Rosicrucian Proverb

The next day Georgie called during Bessie's afternoon nap. Her brother rarely called their mother, and although she was always the one who answered the phone, Dee was never the one he wanted to talk to. His phone conversations never began with a *Hello, Dee, how are you?* Instead, he'd abruptly say, "Let me talk to Ma." And Bessie, when she heard it was her precious son, would practically dance into the kitchen to answer the phone.

"So, Dee," Georgie began, and cleared his throat once before continuing, "How about having lunch with me tomorrow?"

What was going on? He was inviting them to lunch? He never did that. She was suspicious.

But lunch was lunch and it would be good for Bessie, she could ride for days on the good feelings of her beautiful boy taking her out to lunch, smiling and retelling the story until Dee wanted to throw up, or until Bessie completely forgot about the lunch and was back to whining that Georgie never called.

Georgie hadn't said he just wanted Bessie to have lunch with him. Was he including her? That was just weird. She must be mishearing or misunderstanding. She wanted to say, *So what are you up to, Georgie?* Instead she said, "Umm, well, okay, so what time will you be picking her up?"

"Her?" he asked, and was silent for a second before continuing. "No, you're misunderstanding. I'm inviting *you,* just you, to lunch."

"You're not inviting Bessie?"

If their mother ever heard about this she'd be broken-hearted. It was cruel. He must know how Bessie idolized him, how she adored her beautiful boy.

"She'll be so hurt. She should be invited, Georgie. Actually, you should just take Bessie to lunch. It'd make her so happy."

"I'm thinking that you could use a break. I know it can't be easy being alone with Ma full time. It's not easy being with her for ten minutes."

It wasn't easy, but excluding Bessie was wrong.

But.

Buts were twerking inside Dee's brain. *But, damn, I'd really like to go out to lunch, and maybe I've been being unfair to my brother. Maybe he's a good person. Maybe, after all this time, we could be friends, or at least friendly.* She wanted a brother that she could love and care about. She'd love to have a brother that she liked, one that she could call on the phone and say, *How ya doin', Baby Brother. I'm missing you.*

She wanted to go out to lunch. She was curious about him and she really did need a break, but how would she break this to Bessie. No exaggeration, it would be like taking a scalpel and cutting out her mother's heart.

"Georgie," she said. "Bessie would be so hurt. I can't do that to her. I don't think you understand. She can't be left alone. She might put a spoon in the microwave and blow it up. She could wander the neighborhood and get lost or run over by a car. I can't leave her alone."

"Oh, come on, Dee," he said, with the impatience of a man used to getting his way without question. "Ma'll be fine. She still takes an afternoon nap, doesn't she? So, just get her down for a nap and she'll never know you're gone. And anyway, I've asked my girl to come sit with her, so you won't have to worry."

Her brother had a girl? Georgie had no children (that she knew of anyway), so maybe the girl was his secretary? Of course, he'd refer to the woman who was his secretary as his girl.

Now, Dee, she told herself, *give him a break, maybe his secretary is fifteen.*

"Your girl?" she asked, hearing a hint of her mother in her tone.

"My secretary, Ginger," he said, oblivious of her tone. "I've made reservations for us."

Reservations? Before she'd even agreed to join him? But why did that surprise her? Georgie was used to getting his way. And why did she agree to do this? It could create so much trouble. Was she bored, curious, or maybe just hungry for food that she didn't cook?

He said. "Wear something nice, clean."

He was presuming that she'd already said yes. She hadn't agreed yet. And clean? Could she love someone who told her to be clean for lunch? Although, to be fair to him, the last time he showed his face in the house, she had just brought Bessie her bowl of food in the living room, where they liked to watch the news while they ate their dinner in front of the chipped glass coffee table. Bessie had a softly cooked half-chewed carrot in her mouth when she sneezed and sprayed orange bits all over Dee's white blouse. That was when Georgie had dropped by. Was it a year ago? No, probably longer.

If she could get Bessie down for her nap early, she might sleep through and never know Dee had left the house. Bessie usually napped for two or three hours in the afternoon, so against all her best instincts, she agreed to have lunch with her brother.

*

The next day at eleven o'clock Dee made her mother a turkey (oh, lovely lulling tryptophan) with cheese (more tryptophan) sandwich. Plus there was a banana (still more tryptophan), and potato chips (no tryptophan), but Bessie loved chips. She was drugging her mother with food. She was also prepared to lie if Bessie asked why she wasn't eating too. But Bessie, not surprisingly, didn't ask. Food engaged Bessie's full attention. Dee had tied a dish towel around her mother's neck, knowing that spills would happen when Bessie pulled the sandwich apart, taking the lettuce out "for later," although later never came, and stuffing the potato chips between the slices of bread to make it crunchy, losing several chips to the floor and bending to gather them up and spilling more chips as she bent.

Dee gathered up the chips from the floor and started toward the kitchen trashcan to throw them out.

Bessie said, "Wait. Stop. They're perfectly good, they barely touched the floor." So Dee gave Bessie the chips and Bessie put them in her sandwich, but then other chips fell out and hit the floor.

They both laughed, but Dee was getting a stomachache from nerves. She knew she shouldn't have agreed to this lunch with her brother. If Bessie found out that she was seeing Georgie without her, she'd be inconsolable. But worse—though Dee wasn't going to admit to herself that the part that was the worst—was that she'd never hear the end of this major betrayal on her part. Not Georgie's betrayal, only hers.

Georgie was coming at twelve-thirty, and at this rate the damn tryptophan would never reach Bessie's lips. But the sandwich did get eaten. Eventually. And Dee got Bessie on the couch tucked under an afghan, curled up for her nap.

"Play for me, Dee," Bessie said.

This was their routine: Dee would sit at the baby grand piano and play Für Elise, Bessie's favorite lullaby, and before she finished, her mother would be snoring loudly. She found herself rushing notes, as if that would put Bessie to sleep faster, so she forced herself to slow the tempo and hopefully slow the racing of her own heart.

As soon as Dee heard the rumble sound coming from Bessie's nose or opened mouth (she was never sure where the noise came from), she rushed upstairs to change into "clean" clothes. She brushed her hair, aware that she was overdue for a snip and clip here and there all over her head. Oh well, it was just lunch with her brother.

When his car pulled up, his girl, or rather his cute young secretary hopped out and came to the door. She was maybe twenty or possibly thirty, and very pretty with a wholesome red-headed freckledness to her. But *girl?* The older Dee got the harder it was for her to guess anyone's age. Ginger might even be forty.

Dee put her finger to her lips and pointed into the living room at the mound of covers that concealed Bessie. Ginger held up a book, indicating that she'd pass the time reading until they got back.

Then Dee snuck out to Georgie's silver Cadillac.

5. Yellow Roses

"'Tis a fat bird that bastes itself."
Dutch Proverb

The restaurant had white tablecloths with a yellow rose in a glass vase in the center of each table. The rose added to Dee's guilt—it was as if Bessie had chosen the centerpiece.

"Yellow roses are Bessie's favorite," Dee told Georgie, as she fingered the pressed-glass vase.

"Really," Georgie said. "Didn't know she had a favorite. Just figured she liked all plants."

Georgie ordered wine for both of them, pronouncing Chenin Blanc as if he were a French sommelier with a clothespin pinched on his nose. When their drinks came she thanked the waiter. Georgie did not. Did he consider himself so privileged that those who served him didn't deserve a thank you. Underlings. And she was one of them—the waiters, the cooks, the servers, the cashiers, the caretakers, and the daughters. Smaller than him. Less. Never worthy of a thank you.

He held his glass up to her and toasted. "To us," he said.

She smiled and mimicked his words.

"Glad you came," he said.

Question or statement? From his tone she took it as statement.

He was glad she came. Well, maybe they could be friends. She imagined dinners with the family around the old dining room table that was never used anymore. She imagined a picnic in the backyard on the Fourth of July. Hot dogs on the grill, although she doubted that the old grill was still usable. Maybe he would invite Bessie and her to his house, but Georgie could have moved. It seemed ridiculous that she knew so little about her brother.

She asked, "So are you still living in the same house in Beverly Hills?"

"Yep," he said.

"And you had a pool?"

She remembered being at Georgie's house when her husband Sy was still alive. Once. Only once. Maybe they were invited so Georgie could show off his new house? She couldn't remember. Had Bessie and her father been there too? They got the grand tour. From a hall window on the second floor they could see down into the back yard.

As the others in the group moved on to admire the master suite, still standing in the hall, Sy whispered, "Penis," and pointed down at Georgie's pool. She looked down and then giggled into her hand. Yes, the pool was shaped like a penis, long and narrow and curved at the far end for doing laps, the penis effect was enhanced by a hot tub and wading pool closest to the house. She remembered Sy laughing most of the way home, and talking about Liberace having a swimming pool shaped like a piano because he was a pianist. Georgie had a penis shaped pool because he was a dick—Sy couldn't stand Georgie.

"And I do have a pool." Georgie said, "I'm looking forward to opening it up for the summer. Anxious to get back to doing laps."

Her urge to giggle was quickly overcome by grief. Sy (sigh). If Sy were here, how would he respond to Georgie doing laps in his penis pool?

"You look in good shape," she said.

"Beverly Hills Club," he said, and did a one-arm muscle flex.

Were beautiful people more apt to take care of their beautiful bodies? Bessie still did thigh flaps every morning with her back flat on her bed, flapping her knees into each other. What did Dee do? Smoked a cheap cigarette every day, religiously. Her hand came up to her cheek. The tiny red broken veins Bessie had poked at were on the right side, and yeah, she knew it was from smoking. She suddenly felt self-conscious. Homely. She needed to take better care of herself. She couldn't afford a fancy athletic club. Actually, she had tried Bessie's thigh flap thing but she just got bruises on the inside of her knees. She wasn't fat, just a little thick, a bit saggy.

He ordered for both of them, without asking her preference, Cornish hens bathing in a lemon butter sauce. When her lunch arrived she picked at the little bird bones and remembered the bird trapped in the fireplace, all the while worrying about Bessie waking up and finding a strange girl roosting in the house. Why did she agree to do this? Bessie would be so hurt.

And what was this all about? Georgie had never invited her anywhere. They weren't talking, but rather eating silently, like some old married couple, who already knew everything about one another, but in this case, she really didn't know her brother at all.

"So what's new with you?" she asked.

He smiled—deep dimpled and unabashedly happy, and said, "Well, I'm a big brother."

"Really?"

"Yep, I'm a big brother to this kid named Isaiah Thomas."

"The basketball player?"

"Well, of course not the basketball player. This is a kid. No relation to basketball. But, I suppose, probably named after him. I took him fishing." He hesitated then added, "Not fly fishing. We put worms on hooks."

"Georgie, that's really nice. I'm impressed. I thought you didn't like kids."

He was quiet a moment, put his hand to his face, half covering his mouth and muttered, "I would of liked to have had a son."

Georgie had wanted kids; Dee was surprised. She knew his wife, Zita, didn't want children, but it never occurred to her that her brother might. When they were both young women, Zita told Dee that she had decided not to have children because she couldn't stand the thought of stretch marks. *Babies destroy one's figure, don't you know.* Dee had been enormously pregnant at the time of this conversation. Long tendrils of puckered bluish lines ran from her hips to her outie belly button, and Amy, her two-year-old figure destroyer, clung to her legs with sticky fingers.

"So how's Zita?" she asked. This was a good question, sincere. She wasn't even sure he was still married. She had so little contact with her brother that she had no idea what his life was like. He could be on a third or fourth wife by now. The only information she got on him was from him, and he never came around to tell her or his mother anything at all about his life.

"Zita?" he said, and she thought he was about to say, who's Zita? but instead he said, "Zita's fine. Same. Same as always."

"Well, that's good," she said, but was it good? "I'm sorry, Georgie, I didn't know you wanted kids."

Georgie shrugged, and started shoveling food into his mouth as though he were starving.

"So where did you go fishing with Isaiah Thomas? I remember how much you loved fishing with Dad when we were kids. Remember the cottage?"

He didn't respond. Chewed his food and looked irritable. Did she say a wrong thing? She chewed and felt anxious. Guilty. What did she say? And then her guilt morphed back to the leaving Bessie guilt. If Bessie woke up and found her gone...

Georgie said, "How's your hen?"

"Hen?" she was taken aback. She doubted that the city even allowed people to have hens, although fresh eggs would be nice.

He pointed at her plate.

"Oh. Right. It's fine."

She felt stupid. Unnerved. She had forgotten that the dwarf boney little bird on her plate was a hen, and was embarrassed. He was going to think she was losing it. Incompetent. Maybe dementia was setting in.

"So you've been living in our parents' house since the car accident. When was that? Twenty years ago?" he asked.

She shook her head and frowned. It was 1992, the same year her daughter got married, the same year Sy died, the same year she almost died with him, the same year she ended up broken at their parents' house. Why was he bringing it up? If she answered out loud she'd have to finish chewing and swallow first. She swallowed. Coughed.

"More like sixteen years. Why?" she asked. This lunch was such a bad-bad idea. Her stomach was churning.

"I've noticed that the house is looking sorta run down lately?" he said, then sipped his wine. Lately? Had he been doing drive-bys without stopping in to say hi to his mother? *Lately* was more frequent than saying, *today when I picked you up.*

"You probably don't know what the property values are," he continued. He looked smug, all knowing, George Ellison, the pope of mortgages and land values.

Was this it? He invited her to lunch to assess the property value of their parents' house? She swallowed another mouthful of the buttery bird, but neither nodded nor shook her head. Property values were irrelevant to her. He was talking about her, or more accurately, *their* mother's home.

She excused herself and went to the ladies room where fowl sopped in rich sauce left her body in a rush. If she could fly, this was the point where she's go out the restaurant's front door and fly home—be a homing pigeon.

When she returned to the table, she said, "I'm really not feeling well, Georgie. Could we go?"

"What? No dessert or coffee? You were always big on the sweets. Still are, I'd guess."

He had passive aggressive down to an art form.

She shook her head.

He looked at his thick gold watch. "We haven't been gone long at all," He said, in the same whinny voice he'd had as a kid (which usually worked). He looked genuinely disappointed. Maybe he had just wanted her company. Maybe he was just doing something nice for his sister?

"I really don't feel well. I'm sorry," she said.

He waved the waitress over with the efficiency and grace of a prince, and after the credit card business was transacted, he said, "Well, then, let's go."

*

Finally home. She asked him to park up the block so Bessie wouldn't see his car. When she got to the house, she entered the side door soundlessly, and as usual took off her shoes. She crossed her fingers, hoping Bessie was still asleep. It was quiet. She walked barefoot though the house and peeked into the living room where the mound of afghan on the sofa was still covering her mother.

Dee didn't see Ginger anywhere, so she stood still and listened until she heard a faint squeaking sound coming from her father's study. Maybe Georgie's *girl* sat in there to read her book. Smart. Better if Bessie never saw the stranger in the house. She moved quietly to the back room, careful not to wake Bessie.

The door to her father's study was open and she just stood there a moment watching Georgie's secretary shifting through folders in the old file cabinet.

Dee whispered, "If you tell me what you're looking for, maybe I can help you find it."

Ginger jumped and slammed the drawer shut with a loud bang that shook the metal file cabinet. She stammered something about having a nosey tendency.

"My brother's parked down the street," Dee whispered. "Please leave by the side door. Quickly. Quietly."

From the living room, Bessie shouted, "Dee, what was that noise?"

"Everything's fine, Bessie." Dee called, as she hurried Ginger toward the side door.

She watched Ginger run down the driveway. Ginger was very pretty in a wholesome way. She had a beautiful behind, two perfect melons, probably separated by a thong—she had no panty line. Dee watched as Georgie's car pulled up at the end of the driveway; she watched him push the passenger door open from inside; she watched him lean across the front seat and kiss his girl on the mouth.

Watching, Dee made up a poem:

> *Georgie Porgie, puddin' and pie,*
> *kissed the girls to make them sigh,*
> *when his pie was about to bake,*
> *Georgie Porgie wanted cake.*

"What's getting banged," Bessie shouted from the living room. And Dee didn't respond—because it was obvious.

6. CHESS

"That the birds of worry and care fly over your head,
this you cannot change,
but that they build nests in your hair,
this you can prevent."
Chinese Proverb

Dee's children were scattered, blown like dandelion seeds far and away: Amy and her husband Matt and their three kids lived in a hundred-year-old farmhouse outside Montello, Wisconsin, where they were raising grapes and their three children. They had a small winery with several acres rented to a dairy farmer who planted corn for his cows, so their land was also producing the beginnings of Wisconsin cheese—wine and cheese, a perfect pairing.

Dee's son, Paul, had been in and out of Iraq and Afghanistan since 2003, five harrowing fear-filled years. He was a career army major hunting for weapons of mass destruction long after everyone knew there were none. Thinking about her son, Dee felt another twinge about finding the little bird in the fireplace. A bird in the house means someone will die. *Please, please, keep Paul safe,* she whispered, superstitions floating in and out of her head as needed. But, she reminded herself, a week had passed since the bird fell down the chimney and no one had died yet, although an ambulance had screamed down the block one day, and a neighbor they'd never met was taken away on a stretcher. Maybe the bird fell down the wrong chimney?

After their usual post-lunch/pre-nap piano concert in the living room, when Bessie was asleep on the sofa, Dee fixed herself a glass of iced tea, which she carried into her father's mahogany-paneled den to sip while she emailed her daughter Amy. It was a pleasant ritual. Some days she wrote a single sentence, and occasionally (like the occasion after the lunch with Georgie) she had so much to tell that she worried about getting too long winded. But Amy told Dee that she'd be very worried if a day passed without an email from her mother.

When she was finished, she moved to her father's old leather recliner by the window, and stretched out with her ankles crossed—left ankle always felt numb /sleeping/tingly supported by her normal/healthy/ undamaged right ankle.

She picked up her sketchbook and flipped through page after page of her quick pencil sketches of the birds at the feeder outside the window. A few pages had pen drawings of birds, when she pretend to be John James Audubon.

Habits. Order. Afternoons were Dee's favorite time; while her mother napped she could relax and draw the finches and sparrows and robins outside the window (unless she had laundry, dishes, food preparations, dusting or vacuuming).

She had just reached a blank page when the phone rang. She hurried to the kitchen (left ankle not to pleased with the rush) hoping-hoping that the ringing wouldn't wake Bessie. For the eight-hundredth time she wished there was a phone in her dad's study.

"Hey, Dee," a familiar voice said.

"Oh, hey, Ray," she said to Ray Ridgewell, lawyer/lifelong friend. She had gone to grade school with Ray, a nerdy guy who had a crush on her in the sixth grade. When he was a kid, Ray had an untamable cowlick that made him look like Alfalfa in the Little Rascals. The cowlick and all its brown companions were long gone, replaced by a shiny dome of pink skin.

"It's about your brother," Ray said.

"Uh oh, what's Georgie done now?"

"Listen, Dee, there's no real problem, but I wanted to give you a heads-up. Remember that letter you gave me from your brother's attorney?"

Of course, she remembered the letter—a confusing legalize thing that she dropped off at Ray's office on the way to Costco with Bessie. She left Bessie waiting in the car, but then wondered if leaving a woman with dementia alone in the car was as bad as leaving your child there, so she rushed in and out, just leaving the letter with Cara, Ray's assistant.

"I called the guy," Ray said. "He's a real quack. He said that George's suing for his share of your parents' estate."

"What?"

"Don't worry," Ray said. "This lawyer is some sleaze George must have found online, and like I told this so-called lawyer, you can't sue for your share of the estate, if your parents, or parent in this case, is still living. No legitimate lawyer would even consider this case. What puzzles me is that George seems to be a pretty good businessman. I suspect he broached this idea with his own lawyer and got shot down, so then he turned to the yellow pages or went online."

Dee shook her head. Georgie wanted his share. His share? He never shared caretaking, rarely visited, rarely called, although he did send Bessie a card at Christmas and another on her 90th birthday in March, but he wanted his share. There hadn't been a word from him since the fancy lunch. That day, after Ginger, George's secretary had left the house, Dee poked through the file cabinet in her father's office, trying to figure out if Ginger was just nosey, or was actually looking for something. She'd come to no conclusions and had actually forgotten the whole episode.

But now she remembered the drive home from the restaurant when she had lunch with her brother, the lunch that she had naively hoped might be the beginning of a nice relationship with him. When they left the restaurant, Dee knew where they were and she knew where she lived, but he seemed to be orchestrating the ride home like some tune he'd never played before. He headed north, when it was quicker to go South, then made a left turn behind a long line of waiting cars that would take three light changes to complete. He was killing time, giving Ginger more time to search though their father's papers. It wasn't until Ray Ridgewell's call that she realized that Georgie was moving chess pieces in a game she hadn't known they were playing.

Since that day the only time she saw Georgie was on his TV commercials: *This is George Ellison of Ellison Mortgage. Are you worried about qualifying for a loan for that house you've been dreaming of? Don't! Call me and we can set you up with a no documentation loan.*

Even in his old age her brother was still handsome, dashing, his blond hair had gone brown, and now at sixty with some dye (she was sure) it was still brown. With his dimples and innocent blue eyes, he looked honest, trustworthy, but you can't tell a crook by his cover. And now, even though Bessie was still alive, he was after his inheritance.

7. ELEANOR ROOSEVELT

"What is sport to the boy is death to the bird."
Indian Proverb

Georgie, or rather Prince George, was a mean kid. Dee figured it was because he was spoiled rotten. *Oh, little boys are so wonderful, so great. Every mother wants a son.* Dee remembered her parents exclaiming over their new baby boy, even her father. *We have a son to carry on the family name. If I had known babies were so great, I'd had them sooner and more of them.*

She was five. They'd had a kid for four years before Master Wonderful arrived, but she wasn't all that great, she was just a girl, chinless with sticky-out ears and buck teeth, not pretty like her brother or mother, or for that matter even her father, who was a nice looking man with kind blue eyes and a tidy goatee. She used to wonder if they'd found her on the front porch abandoned in a laundry basket along with some stranger's dirty socks.

Dee was a good girl: quiet, obedient. Sometimes they didn't realize she was in the room with them, so she heard things they probably wouldn't have wanted her to hear. When she was twelve, she overheard Bessie telling someone on the phone that Dee looked like she could have been Eleanor Roosevelt's child.

Hopeful, Dee pulled out the R volume of The Encyclopedia Britannica in her father's study and read everything she could find about the former First Lady. When she first saw the photos of Mrs. Roosevelt, she pressed the page to her newly budding chest and hugged the heavy book. Then, whenever she felt insecure or ugly or just not good enough, she'd sneak the book into her bedroom—no one noticed it was missing from the shelf in her father's study—and reread passages about Eleanor Roosevelt.

She decided not to worry about being pretty; instead she was going to be a kind and wonderful person, beautiful—just like Grandma Eleanor. Oh, yes, Dee had decided that Eleanor Roosevelt was her real grandmother. When she was old enough, she was going to change her name to Delores Roosevelt. Every Saturday morning she wrote a letter to Mrs. Roosevelt, she told her all her troubles, told her of incidents in school when someone said something hurtful to her. But she also told her about the good things, like the new teacher in her art class.

She pondered in one letter, could it be that when she and Grandma Eleanor were forming inside their mothers' bodies that something had gone wrong, and whatever it was that made chins, had all gone toward making big teeth?

She wanted to be just like Eleanor, caring for people, especially less fortunate people. Maybe she'd be a nurse for the Red Cross. She'd go overseas when there was a war, and work in a white tent with a big red plus sign on the roof. She'd bandage soldiers, talk to them kindly, and then the soldiers would fall in love with her, for herself, no matter what she looked like. They would love her, because she loved them, because she was gentle and listened to their troubles and patted their hands. But wait, what if they'd lost their hands in the war? Well, then she'd pat their cheeks and smooth their hair away from their eyes. She'd listen, really listen, and not just look like she was listening to whatever they had to say. Goodness, warmth, and charity would spill out of her.

Each Saturday morning when her brother was downstairs being swooned over by her mother, watching cartoons and laughing his silly head off, and getting his breakfast delivered to him on a teak tray in the living room, Dee was up in her pink bedroom writing to Grandmother Eleanor. When a letter was finished, she'd add it to the bundle that was tied with a pink ribbon and hidden in the back of her underwear drawer. They were never mailed.

She wanted to volunteer at a soup kitchen, but her request was denied. The Ellison's young daughter would definitely not be going into some ghetto. It could be dangerous out there in the big world. *No, if you want to do something, you can get a babysitting job. In fact, when your mother has to be somewhere, you can watch your little brother.* Most of her friends with siblings had babysat the younger kids, but Bessie never liked leaving Georgie behind. When her parents went out for an evening, Mrs. Platt, a nice woman who'd squeeze them in massive hugs against her body that was as soft as a pile of down pillows, would watch them both. Dee liked the hugs, except sometimes she got entangled with her nose near Mrs. Platt's overly perfumed armpit.

So, okay, here's a test for Eleanor Roosevelt's granddaughter: could she be kind and understanding to her nasty eight-year-old brother. She was twelve—that meant that she was mature and responsible. She decided that she was up for the challenge, so on a Saturday when her mother was going grocery shopping, Dee offered to watch Georgie.

Her mother was a bit disappointed, she liked having her beautiful son with her, but after Bessie had cooed and clucked over leaving her baby boy behind, she trotted out the front door and got into her Lincoln and drove off.

Dee made Georgie a peanut butter and jelly sandwich, which she put on a plate at the kitchen table. She poured him a glass of milk, and then watched, appalled, as he ripped the sandwich apart, all the while screaming at her, "Mommy cuts my crusts off! You're an ugly turd. Don't you know anything about anything? You don't even know how to cut crusts off bread. Stupid Girl!" He shoved the torn hunks of bread into his glass of milk, still screaming. The milk ran over the top of the glass and she ran for a dishrag to clean up the mess.

She was trying to be nice. What would Eleanor Roosevelt do?

Dee apologized to her hateful little brother, "I'm sorry, Georgie. I'll make you a new sandwich," she said. "I'll cut the crusts off."

But it was too late, he ran off smearing his milky peanut buttered hands on the walls as he raced through the house. She chased him, but he reached the first floor lavatory ahead of her and locked himself in. Even without putting her ear to the door, she could hear the water running. The toilet flushed. And still the water was running. He was going to flood the bathroom and she'd be the one in trouble. She beat her fists on the door, screamed at him to turn the water off, come out of there NOW! But the door didn't open and the water was still running.

And then she heard someone come in the front door. *Oh, no, was Bessie back already?*

But no, it was Georgie. He'd climbed out of the bathroom window, ran around to the front door, and was running through the house taunting her. He ran into the kitchen and grabbed the plate she'd put his sandwich on. He waved it in the air, with crumbs and the remains of his sandwich flying all over.

"I'm gonna smash this plate and tell Mommy that you threw it at me."

Without hesitation, he threw Bessie's supposedly unbreakable plastic plate against the wall, cracking it in half and leaving a nasty scrape mark where it hit. Dee was relieved that she had chosen one of the plain old kitchen plates that had scratch marks. Then, as Georgie was snickering, and enjoying the mess he made, she grabbed him, and held him from behind as he kicked and jerked and smashed his heels into her shins.

She whispered in his ear. "You're a nice boy. You want to be nice. Please be nice." She whispered over and over the things she wanted to be herself, things Eleanor Roosevelt would like her to be, whispered until finally he gave in and stopped kicking and screaming. But she kept it up, holding him tight, "You want to be a nice person. You want to be good." He was sweaty. She could smell the saltiness of his skin, and the wet dog stinkiness of him. His hair was plastered to his forehead. Then thinking about the soldier she'd help one day, she moved one of her hands up to gently remove the damp hair from his eyes. That's when he broke loose, swung around and punched her in the face.

Then he was running again, but this time upstairs to his bedroom, she halfway hoped he'd jump out of his bedroom window, but then she'd really be in trouble. She didn't follow. The water was still running in the bathroom. She ran outside and looked up at the first floor lavatory window. Georgie had jumped down without hurting himself. She got a ladder from the garage, and nervously climbed up and into the opened window. There was nearly a half-inch of water on the floor, held in by the sill at the door. She turned off the faucet and used towels to mop up the water, ringing them out in the sink.

By the time Bessie got home Dee had cleaned up the peanut butter smeared walls and had thrown out the broken pieces of plate. Her eye had swollen up where he punched her and her bruised shins ached.

When Georgie heard his mother come in the house he came running down the stairs and cried, "Mommy, Mommy, don't ever leave me with her again. She's mean to me."

Bessie pinched her lips together and gave Dee the evil eye all the while shaking her head and looking disappointed.

"She locked me in the bathroom, Mommy," her brother said between hiccupping sobs.

"But the bathroom doesn't lock from the outside," Dee said.

With his arms around Bessie's hips, looking innocently up into his mother's eyes, Georgie whined, "Then she was holding the door shut, so I couldn't get out. I was so scared, Mommy."

Dee was sent to her room, where she wrote another letter to Eleanor Roosevelt.

When her father came home from his golf game later that day, he was upset about Dee's black eye. In his gentle way, he had her sit beside him on the sofa, he asked her to tell him exactly what happened. And so she did. She told him in detail about the flooded bathroom and the smashed plate, and how she'd held her brother and said calming words to him and how he had kicked her. Here (as part of the show and tell) she stretched her legs out, so he could see her bruised shins.

When Dee had told all she had to tell, her father had shouted, "George Ellison, you get in here right this minute."

There was no response.

Weary, not at all pleased about this whole matter, her father got up and strode into the kitchen where Georgie was clinging to Bessie's side, "Get over here, you're going to the woodshed."

Woodshed? What did that mean? They didn't have a woodshed. But her father, still dressed up like a golf clown in his bright yellow slacks and pink shirt and white golf shoes, took a firm grip on Georgie's skinny arm and lead him to the basement door. When he opened the door, he told Dee to come too and ordered Bessie to stay right where she was.

Dee followed her father and brother down the stairs. She watched her father pull down Georgie's pants and remove the shiny white patent leather belt from his yellow pants. He folded the belt in half and raised his arm high, stopped, looked at Dee with a question mark on his face. She was in shock, frozen motionless. Then the belt came down and wacked Georgie's pink butt once. Of course, Georgie screamed, and then Bessie was at the top of the stairs screaming too. Then her father screamed at his wife to go back to the kitchen. Dee stood there soundless with her mouth wide opened. Her father looked at her, studied her a moment and then struck pink flesh once more. Then he looked at Dee.

"Enough?"

She nodded, and then ran up two flights of stairs to her room.

It wasn't what she wanted her father to do. Her brother looked so terrified and little and vulnerable. She didn't want him to get hurt. She wanted him scolded or confined to his room, not hit. But why hadn't she stopped her father after the first whack? As soon as she saw her father remove his belt, she could have said, "No, don't." but she didn't. And so it was laid on her. Her father was just doing what he thought she wanted. Her brother's beating was laid in her lap. Nothing was solved. Georgie would hate her all the more, and her mother probably did too, and her father was surely disappointed in the kind of person she was. SHE was the big person who whipped a little kid.

She vowed that she would never tell on Georgie again. And because she was ashamed, she didn't write Eleanor Roosevelt about the beating either.

*

Dee had broken a few vows in her lifetime, none of great consequence (at least that she could, or chose to, remember), but now she broke the vow never to tell on Georgie. She told her attorney, Ray Ridgewell, about her lunch with Georgie, and how his secretary had searched through her father's files.

Ray said, "Okay, Dee. Stay alert. Who knows what he'll try next. And maybe we should get together with your mother, the three of us. You need to have power of attorney and guardianship for her. So let's do that soon."

8. LEFT BROKEN

"A bird never flew on one wing."
Danish Proverb

Dee would try to stay alert, try to stay one step ahead of her brother. But would she even remember to stay alert after a month had passed? She could put a note on her bedroom wall. "Be on your toes around your brother." How would she interpret that note months into the future? If Georgie didn't come around for another year or more, would she think staying on her toes had to do with being a dancer in the Nutcracker Suite? She smiled picturing herself in pink satin toe shoes. Could she even twirl on one foot? She laughed out loud, and said, "Yeah, right."

She had tucked Bessie in for the night with a glass of water on her night table, her dentures in a glass, the last pee performed, the Depends in place, the nightlight on, and the door left open a crack.

Finally, Dee stretched out on her bed. Not the twin bed she'd had in her childhood, which her parents had replaced after she left home and eloped with Sy Chope. They had tastefully decorated her old bedroom with a double bed to accommodate out-of-town relatives. But still it was the same room, in the same house, on the same street where she grew up. The sameness of it all was exhausting and comforting.

When she came home after the accident, and when she was well enough to climb the stairs, she moved back into her old bedroom. Once her childhood bedroom had been pink and frilly and loaded with clutter: posters, a shelf full of dolls, tea sets, and collections of things that she had once loved. But after she married, she had packed her youth into boxes that she moved to her own adult home, and later she passed her girly treasures down to her daughter, Amy. The missing item from her childhood was a replica of the family's cottage that her father had built for her. It had been there in the corner of her room when she went away to college, but when she came home, it was gone.

Eventually, she removed the Marimekko fabric from the room's walls, the huge pattern's loudness overwhelmed her, and then she painted everything white. It was a blank canvas where her mind could rest. The old dresser painted white merged into the white walls. Her blanket, all her bedding, was white. The creaking floorboards were brown but that was okay, they grounded her space. It was a quiet monastic space. When she did her bird drawings they went into the bottom drawer of her dresser or stayed in her sketchbooks, and were never hung on the walls. The quiet room was her sanctuary ever since the car accident.

*

The car accident...

Dee's husband, Sy Chope, had given their daughter Amy away to Matt Baker on Saturday, June 20, 1992. A month later on the way home from his parent's anniversary party in Lansing, Sy, in effect, gave Dee back to her parents.

It was three in the morning, when, thank goodness, traffic was minimal. According to a witness and the police, Sy was driving like a hot-rodding teenager when he crashed through the rails of an overpass. The car did an Olympic dive, trunk rolling over hood before landing on it's left side on the highway below. He was killed and Dee was left broken: left leg, left arm, and her brain had smashed against the left side of her skull when her head slammed into her husband's. Jaws of life pulled the crushed car parts away from her broken body.

For ten days her lights were out. She was in a coma. Her daughter, Amy, drove home from Wisconsin with her brand new husband, and her son, Paul, newly commissioned in the army, came home on emergency leave. Later Dee was told that her kids had taken turns reading *To Kill a Mockingbird* to her, although she had no memory of it, or even of seeing either of them. A month passed before Dee was transferred to a nursing home.

Two months later she was released into her parents' care and they brought her home.

Her father set her up with a rented hospital bed in his study—a dim room on the north side of the house—but most important it was on the main floor and she wouldn't have to the climb stairs. The room was rearranged so she could watch the birds at the feeder from the bed.

After the accident, Bessie became the mother that Dee had always wanted. Bessie took her to physical therapy sessions, speech therapy, doctors and more doctors, while her father worked his usual long hours.

There was a time when she was still barely able to speak when she woke to find Bessie sitting on her Dad's recliner next to her bed. She was crying.

Still struggling with language and words not completely formed, Dee said, "What if your face gets stuck like that, and you get inkles?" Immediately Bessie's face went neutral, but then she laughed and came over to the bed and kissed Dee. It was one of Dee's all time best memories.

Bessie, who was always a homebody and loved projects, made Dee her project. But it was more than that, Bessie was quietly patient as she darned tiny stitches in the hole of Dee's memory. She helped her learn to read again, quietly waiting for her daughter to find the word that was locked away in some drawer or cupboard in her brain. Bessie had had migraines when she was a young woman, and Dee thought that was how her mother knew the house should be kept dim and sounds quiet in those early months of Dee's recovery.

During the first months after the car accident Sy's parents had called a few times, but she was confused on the phone, had no notion who they were, her brain was still in malfunction mode. In the beginning they sent get-well cards, but after a while it was like they never existed or maybe she didn't. When they had Sy's funeral she was still in a coma, and she had never been to his gravesite. Sometimes she thought about going, but driving a hundred miles to Lansing (where his parents lived and owned a family plot in a cemetery) would be like driving to Hawaii only less soggy.

Months after his death, she remembered that Sy had wanted to be cremated, not buried, but what was she supposed to do about it then. He had told her that he was more afraid of bugs eating him, than fire. Funny, a big man like Sy screaming for her to save him from a spider. It happened many times. She always rushed to his rescue, and using her bare thumb, squashed the nasty bug. It gave her a sense of power, a feeling of cocky smugness that she tried not to show this man who was smarter, faster and stronger than her. He had even been a wiz at diaper changing and storytelling when their kids were little. His only weakness was spiders (and loving fast cars). But his parents made the choice—they buried him and fed him to the creepy crawlies. She had lost control of her life and his eternity.

After the accident Dee felt there were things she had forgotten, and for months she begged her mother to tell her what it was. It felt like something important. There was a vague, yet nagging sense of something she needed to know, but Bessie just looked puzzled like she didn't know what it could be, shook her head, told her not to fret and just be glad to be alive. Sometimes she still felt that she had forgotten something, but came to the conclusion that the blank space in her brain—that once held childhood history lessons—was just a shadow space, a black hole where no thoughts lived, and if she came too close to its edges she might be sucked in and then she'd forget all the things she had struggled so hard to remember.

One thing she remembered from that time was Georgie coming into the study where she slept in the hospital bed, and telling her that he thought that Sy drove over the overpass on purpose, that Sy had intended to kill them both. She was still muddled, fuzzy and in pain, why would Georgie tell her that? It was cruel and she chose not to believe him.

But still he had put a question mark in her head—a mean thought that contaminated what she knew was true. On many occasions during their life together, Sy had fantasized about driving a race car like Mario Andretti. He liked speed. Maybe he was just traction sampling his new car. Drag racing. Maybe he was hot rodding like a menopausal male, showing off his fast new car to her or himself. He'd just bought the Corvette. New. Brand new.

It was yellow, a color for school buses and caution lights. He wasn't trying to kill them. Sy had been happy.

Georgie told her that there had been a mist of rain that night, and any race car driver or new owner of a muscle car would know that that was when the road was slickest and most dangerous.

Was Georgie jealous because she was getting so much attention from their parents?

Sy had been happy.

Did she ask her father about it? She was almost certain that she did, *almost* certain that she had asked her father if he thought Sy had been trying to kill them both, without mentioning Georgie (there was the woodshed to consider even when Georgie was full grown.) And in her fuzzy memory (or maybe it was a script she wrote herself) her father had said, "Never. Sy was a good man. He would never knowingly hurt you. He loved you, Dee. You could see it on his face when you'd come into a room. It was such a look of relief and happiness." It was something that her father would have said, because he was a kind gentle man and he loved her. She knew that.

But over the years she found herself, while washing the dishes, or folding clothes, hearing a voice in her head, say, "No, Georgie, you're wrong. Sy was happy." It happened often and at odd times. There was an aura of insecurity in the statement. Why did she have to keep reassuring herself? Maybe it was just a habit? If so, it was worse than smoking.

How could she not hate her brother? He was cruel and mean and life was already hard enough.

9. Angels on High

*"Some birds are not meant to be caged
their feathers are too bright and they're meant to fly."*
African Proverb

Two years before the accident, Dee and Sy Chope bought a house in Indian Village in Detroit. They sold their suburban Birmingham house for a small fortune—location, location, location—when their kids had completed their public school educations and were off to college, and invested in a house that was twice as big and a quarter of the cost in Detroit. They'd been on tours of several restored homes in Indian Village, a neighborhood diverse in age and race, friendly, with a strong community spirit. It fit their dreams and wasn't far from their jobs in the Renaissance Center on the Detroit River. They bought the house to restore it and make it beautiful again. They bought the house because they believed in Detroit, believed that the city, just like their new old house, was worth loving. They sanded and polished the old woodwork. They scrubbed and painted the gentleman's smoking room and the ladies' parlor. Mostly the house wanted a bath, a good scrubbing behind its ears, and a new roof.

They met their neighbors and planned on getting involved in the annual yard/garage sale, but first the house had to be made livable. When work at their day jobs slowed down and the house didn't require every extra minute of their free time, they planned to do things and become more involved in this lovely community. Except for Sondra and William next door, they were too busy to get to know most of their neighbors beyond a hello or a smiling nod.

One Saturday, when art director Sy was off somewhere in Colorado on a photo shoot of Lincolns with a mountain backdrop, Dee was up on a ladder washing years of grimy orange/brown cigar smoke stains off the ten-foot high entry hall ceiling. She uncovered pale blue that looked like sky, and then a white wing. She was so excited she almost fell off the ladder. Carefully, gently, lightly, slowly washing, she exposed an angel and fluttering bluebirds hovering on the high ceiling. She ran next door and got Sondra to come and see what some wannabe Michelangelo had painted decades ago.

"Girl, I think you've found heaven in your hallway. That angel's there to protect you," Sondra said.

Too bad there wasn't an angel painted on the ceiling of Sy's yellow Corvette.

But then after the accident, and being without Sy (sigh), and being as banged up as she was, the Indian

Village house was more than she could manage, so her father sold it. Movers brought everything she owned and piled it all in the Ellison basement—every physical inanimate object left from her marriage and twenty years of raising her children was packed into her parents cellar.

Although Dee and Sy had only restored the first floor, and replaced the roof, the money left from the sale of the Birmingham house and the Indian Village house gave her enough to pay off the mortgage and the hospital bills that weren't covered by insurance, plus a small nest egg for her retirement or a rainy day.

Dee stayed on with her parents. They were her angels—sweet and gentle. Her mother (the same woman who had locked her in the dog run when she was little) was kind, patient, and loving. And now, even though there were times she was exasperated with Bessie's repetitions and confusion, she could reach inside herself and remember when she was the one with the lost thoughts.

Before the accident she had been a commercial artist, specifically a penciler. Her girlhood fantasy of being a nurse for the Red Cross never came to fruition, mainly due to her inability to conquer science, and her obsessive need to draw pictures. In fact, when she was taking a basic biology class in her first year at Michigan State, the instructor asked if she planned to go into nursing. She gathered that he didn't think it was the best plan, so she said, "No." He said, "That's good, then you'll pass this class with a C." When she had completed three years at

State, she came back to Detroit to study commercial art at the College for Creative Studies.

She found a job in the mat room in one of the city's advertising studios and eventually became a penciler. Most studios had one or two pencilers, but she was probably the only female penciler in town. She worked in a studio that serviced ad agencies in the Renaissance Center on the Detroit River, where she drew engines and chassis for auto brochures in fine thin pencil lines. An alternator, an idle-speed solenoid, an exhaust recirculating valve, the oil dipstick, an ignition wire, the spark-plug boots, the heat riser belt were important pieces of a whole that someone could study when buying a new car. When the art directors from the advertising agencies in the Renaissance Center—Y&R, or J. Walter Thompson and their clients—usually Ford—approved of her work, it was passed on to one of the guys in the studio to be airbrushed.

That was where she met, worked with, dated, fell in love with, and married art director, Sy Chope.

She had thought (before the accident) that her main task was to simplify and organize images, so a car buyer looking at a Lincoln catalog would see the distinct internal workings of the car. She thought it was like being a medical illustrator—showing how all a patient's internal organs fit together. But after the accident tasks that had never been complicated before overwhelmed her. Her own thoughts were too fuzzy to clarify even the simplest object for someone else.

Do one thing at a time, Dee. Take notes and concentrate on one thing at a time. The therapists told her to keep a notebook—writing things down would help her memory, but it wasn't long before the words became little drawings and the healing sped up. A year later she went back to work at the studio, back to drawing dashboards, chassis and engines.

10. JACK

*"Don't admire the flying bird
before you know the pain of flapping."*
African Proverb

When her grief over Sy's death had become acceptance, and her body and brain were like a refurbished used car that still had a bent chassis—though to look at it you'd never guess—she started to search for an apartment. She was ready to be back on her own—in her own place—with all the treasured things that she had in her parents' basement. And she'd get a kitten, a little fuzz ball that she'd name Fiona. Fiona was the name she chose for her daughter Amy, but Sy had hated it. He also wasn't fond of cats. So now she was free to get a kitty. In losing so much, there might be new things to find.

Her parents could go back to their bridge foursomes with friends and the expensive dinners with clients that her Dad loved. They could all move forward or back independently, whichever way they wanted to go. She could afford an apartment, maybe one along the Detroit

River where she could watch boats gliding over the deep water and look across to Canada. If her new apartment had a balcony she could watch fireworks being shot from barges as Detroit and Windsor celebrated Canada Day and Independence Day on the river. She was ready, and she told herself that her parents were ready to have their mended bird fly out of the nest.

But after working late at the studio one night—it was summer and all the car catalogs came out in the fall, which meant everyone was cranking out creativity, past the cocktail hour, past dinner, and past the late night TV shows—she came home and found her father unconscious in a pool of blood in the first floor lavatory. Dee's father, Jack Ellison, had an ulcer problem that he tried to wash away with Tums and martinis—very dry (the martinis, not the Tums). An ambulance raced him to the hospital where they removed three-quarters of his stomach. He lost a lot of blood—quarts, or maybe it was gallons.

Later the surgeon came into the waiting room and told Bessie and Dee that Jack had died on the operating table, but the doctor refused to let him go. He didn't give up. With barely containable pride, he told Jack's loved ones of the miracle he had performed.

Before long Jack Ellison came home.

Maybe it was because he had died and oxygen stopped feeding his brain, or maybe it was the whole body trauma, or maybe it would have happened anyway—but Jack Ellison's memory slipped over the next year. At first they were barely aware that anything was wrong, but it soon became obvious that Jack was losing Jack.

He lost his good job, and then a mediocre job. He made mistakes at work enough times that eventually there wasn't any work for him. One morning he got dressed up in his suit and tie, forgetting that his uniform was no longer business formal, and now involved a red vest for his job as a store greeter. When he got into his car, he forgot how to turn the key, so he stayed home that day and from then on.

Jack tried not to lose Jack when he went shopping at Oakland Mall with Bessie. "Meet me in the center of the mall," Bessie told him. He sat on a bench the whole time she was gone, afraid that if he moved, he'd forget where he was supposed to be.

Dee took on her father's role, going to work and paying all the bills, including a second mortgage on the house—she wanted to be charitable but still resented that one. Her father had always had a decent job, but evidently an expensive lifestyle—expensive dinners with clients, a golf club membership. But what else? Was he gambling or something? She remembered several years before when Jack had invited the whole family (Sy and her and the kids, and Georgie and his wife, Zita) out to dinner at a fancy restaurant to celebrate having paid off his mortgage. She still couldn't figure out why he owed so much money. Bottom line: her father had been living beyond his means, and she was paying for his fun while having no fun herself—no lunches out with her coworkers, no drinks after work, no cute new clothes. Her entertainment was clipping coupons, and hunting for markdowns. But she did it—she paid the bills. She owed him. It had nothing to do with finances and everything to do with love.

Bessie took care of Jack. Her mother's patience with her father was inspiring, except for the ice. Her father had always been brilliant, a math wiz, a wordsmith—a man who could have been a million dollar winner on Jeopardy. But after he was physically healed, Jack sat for long hours jiggling ice cubes—tinkle-tinkle—in his glass of water, while he struggled with simple crossword puzzle books. The tinkle noise drove Bessie crazy. It made her cranky. Dee wondered at the time if Bessie was really irritated about the clinking of ice cubes in her father's glass, or was she pissed-off that Jack actually seemed blasé—staying home drinking water when he was supposed to be the bread-winner.

Bessie threw out all the ice cube trays, and within a couple days, Jack forgot that he liked ice in his water. Bessie's irritation dissolved and she never mentioned that this wasn't the husband she had expected to end up with. She kept her face neutral.

Dee's father, who had once been warm and charming, genuinely interested in anyone he came in contact with—the perfect salesman—became suspicious and deceitful. He hid candy bars, afraid that Dee would take them. He hid his toothbrush—same reason. Dee might have been interested in the candy, but his toothbrush? When Jack forgot his hiding places, Dee would be in trouble. He'd shout at her, becoming someone she had never known before.

At Halloween she bought a couple bags of Hershey bars (his favorite) that she kept in her underwear drawer—never mind that she went around smelling like chocolate, and all the male artists at the studio praised her new perfume "Eau Du Chocolat"—but when her father searched the house for a candy bar that he had probably eaten himself, she'd hand him a Hershey and say, "Oh, Dad, were you looking for this?"

One Christmas, Dee's children—daughter Amy, her husband Matt, the first two of the eventual three grandchildren, and her son Paul—were all able to come home for the holiday. They were having a big family dinner around the dining room table. Bessie had baked a tray full of russet potatoes and rather than pass a heavy bowl around the table, Dee took the bowl to the dining room and put one potato on each plate. Jack's interest had devolved to basic survival—food. He barely spoke any more and was always searching for something to eat, and yet he was so thin that it seemed like his body didn't recognize nourishment.

As Dee walked around the table putting a potato on each plate, her father was right behind her stuffing the scalding hot potatoes into his pants pockets. He had gotten one into each pocket when Dee rushed to him to remove the hot potatoes before he was burnt. It was clear that he didn't feel the heat. He cried when she took the potatoes, and she brought him into the kitchen and sat him down with a bowl of dry Cheerios to tide him over until the rest of the meal was ready.

Eventually her father forgot how to walk. Next he forgot how to chew. Bessie would put his complete meals in the blender until they were a soupy mush, then she'd spoon the goop into his mouth, and tell him to swallow. When he forgot how to breath he died in his own bed with his mouth wide open trying to find oxygen.

Dee still missed her father. It was sad to realize that she missed him even more when he was still alive—during those last years of his life, roaming lost and confused around the house, a person she didn't know—than she missed him after he was really gone.

When Jack's ulcer exploded, Dee stopped looking at apartments. Dee's income paid off the second mortgage on her parents' house; she paid the taxes, the utilities, and bought the groceries. Her family needed her. After Jack died Bessie started wandering through the shadow land of lost memory, a familiar place to Dee. They all needed one another—each one taking a turn. Dee couldn't leave Bessie alone, so stayed home and did what freelance work she could.

Was Dee throwing in the towel at the last stop in the road of life? Yep. As long as there were two of them alive and kicking, tripping, sipping, yipping and yapping, she'd be living with and caring for Bessie, and feeling tired most of the time.

11. SINGING

"A bird does not sing because it has an answer.
It sings because it has a song."
Chinese proverb

After the accident it took a while before she was allowed to drive, but eventually her reaction time was tested, and the therapist said she could get on the road again. She wasn't ready. She was afraid that she might be a danger to someone else—she never wanted to hurt anyone the way she had been hurt. But eventually she wanted a new sketchpad, something she'd need to choose herself. Besides, she craved the smell of colored pencils and the feel of watercolor paper, so she got in the car and drove to the art supply store.

Now she drove around the Northern Detroit suburbs on excursions of hunting and gathering, and it was always-always-always with Bessie. When they went to Costco, she had to keep a reign on her. She had her mother push the grocery cart for stability, her beloved black cane stuck in the basket. Bessie loved the samples of food being handed out. She was always anxious to see *the feeders*, as she called the men and women handing out samples from their metal carts. But when her appetite waned she'd put the treats in her coat pockets: cheese and ham and cookies and chips saved for later. Once Dee stopped her a second before she tried to put a plastic cup of chicken pot pie in her coat pocket. She kept a sharp watch on Bessie when they were near any of the sample stations, but she didn't stress about it too much after she bought Bessie a jacket that she could throw in the washing machine, a pocket full of squished sponge cake was messy, but it wasn't worth getting excited over.

The Costco membership was an extravagance, scrimping as they did, but the big space was perfect for getting in some walking on a flat surface in all kinds of weather, and Bessie loved the snacks.

Costco was their athletic club and their entertainment.

Movies didn't work, they were expensive, but an equal problem was Bessie's loud conversations with the characters on the screen. She'd even done that when Dee was just a kid. Her mother always had to add her two cents. "Look out, he's behind you," she'd shout out when the bad guy arrived on the scene, or "so kiss her already," in a languishing love scene. Her father had stopped taking them to the movies after they all sat in some musical, which Bessie took as an occasion for a sing-along.

Dee remembered Bessie singing when she cooked, singing when she dusted, and singing very loud, projecting like she was in the Detroit Opera House while pushing the noisy Hoover around. There were lullabies, sung in a near whisper as she sat beside Dee in the hospital bed waiting for her daughter to be whole again after the accident.

Had Bessie ever dreamt of being a famous singer? Dee asked her mother years ago, around the time when she herself was well enough to go back to work, if Bessie was disappointed with her life. Didn't she dream of being a professional singer? And Bessie had looked startled at the idea of such a thing.

"You sing like a bird, Bessie," Dee had said. Then she wondered if that made it sound like Bessie tweeted, warbled, cawed or chirped?

"You girls now, all so ambitious. Why, Dee, when I was growing up my father came home from work and laid his paycheck in my mother's lap."

Dee wondered what that had to do with singing, but said, "So you wanted paychecks laid in your lap?"

"No, I wanted a good husband."

"You wanted a rich husband."

"Well, of course. Why would I want a poor husband?"

"And powerful?"

"That would've been nice too. A senator."

"Were you disappointed that dad wasn't powerful? A senator? Governor? President of the United States?"

"No, Dee, your father was a good provider. I have a lovely house. I was cared for, I was what I wanted to be, and I sing because I like singing."

Bessie had a limited delineation of what a woman could and should be. Earlier in April, during the debates between Obama and Clinton, Bessie said she couldn't imagine the dilemma for the Democrats having to choose a black man or a woman. Neither would be qualified for president in Bessie's estimation. She was relieved that she was a Republican and could vote for a white man.

Dee said. "I'd be happy with either of the Democrats."

"Dee, listen to you, that tone of voice. You're so arrogant."

What tone of voice, Dee wondered? She didn't hear any arrogance in her voice.

"Thinking you're so right," Bessie went on. "You're so self-righteous. And you act like my opinions are stupid. Like I'm some demented old woman. Just so's you know. I am not stupid."

"I don't agree with you. How is that acting arrogant? When you disagree with what I say, you walk out of the room. You, Bessie, you don't respect me, or my opinions."

Bessie's opinions were firm and strong. Dee's opinions were firm and strong and the exact opposite of her mother's. How do you live with someone whose opinion you disagree with? Do you just avoid the areas of contention? And if you can't speak without fighting how do you get to understand each other. How do you do that in an election year? Occasionally they argued, and then realizing they'd never change each other's mind, they'd shut up and go back to talking about the non-conflict subjects—weather and groceries.

12. A DOG IN THE HOUSE

"It's only a mad dog that barks at a flying bird."
African Proverb

Sunday nights were special—every week Bessie and Dee looked forward to their Sunday night TV shows. "Brothers and Sisters" was the favorite. Dee made a big bowl of popcorn, and then they sat beside each other on the sofa absorbed in the drama. Dee found Sally Fields' large family enviable. They were all so close, always backing each other up, phoning, lunching, having massive family dinners, and rushing to each other's aid. They were fighting and dealing with trauma, but always in the end they were a close loving family. It was enviable. Sally Field was a widow in the show. Dee was also a widow. If her children lived close by, would they come for Sunday night dinners? Would they play games together? Yahtzee? Trivial Pursuit? Scrabble? Charades? Bessie was also a widow, and her children barely spoke to each other.

Suddenly Bessie grabbed Dee's hand and squeezed hard.

"Did you let that dog in the house, Dee? Why's that dog in the house? I'm afraid, Dee!" Her voice rose with her escalating fear. "Why's a dog in the house?" Now she was screaming.

"What dog?" Dee asked.

"Right over there, Dee. Right in front of the TV set. A big brown dog. See! See?"

Dee got up and stood in the spot where Bessie pointed.

"Here?" she said, as gently as she could, feeling afraid, but not of dogs. "Bessie, there's no dog in the house."

"It was there. Now it's gone. I swear, Dee. I saw a huge brown dog." And then she started to cry. Between sniffles she asked, "Am I going crazy?"

"Probably," Dee said. She wrapped her arms around Bessie and held her.

"It's not my fault. Just so's you know, it's Petey's fault I'm going crazy."

"Who's Petey?"

"Oh, come on, Dee, I told you about Petey before."

"I don't remember any Petey."

"Ha! So you're losing your marbles too."

Bessie crossed her arms and looked smug.

"So who's Petey already? Geez."

"Dee! You know you shouldn't say that word." Geez came awfully close to saying Jesus, which should never be used in a negative way.

Dee didn't respond, but in her head she screamed, GEEZ!

"I know I told you before...lots of times, Dee. Petey was my mother's parakeet. I hated that bird, he'd get out of his cage and fly around the house and swoop down and land on my head and peck at my brains. Just so's you know...it's Petey fault that I was seeing that dog."

Dee *had* heard the parakeet stories before.

"Maybe your mother sprinkled birdseed on your head?" Dee suggested. "Or maybe Petey was just making a nest in your beautiful hair?"

"It was very beautiful, just so's you know."

"Do you feel like watching the rest of the show?"

"Well, I sure don't want to miss it. Besides the dog went home." Bessie said.

"Well, mostly we just missed the commercials. The dog's timing was perfect." With her arm back around Bessie, Dee said, "Maybe we should keep some dog biscuits handy, in case it comes back?"

"Don't be a smarty pants. I was really scared." Bessie said.

*

Later, after Bessie was in bed for the night, Dee called her daughter—it was an hour earlier in Wisconsin.

"Bessie saw a brown dog in the house," she told Amy.

"Dog? When did you get a dog, Mom?"

"We don't have any dog. No, Amy, she was hallucinating. I'm really worried."

"You should take her to a doctor."

"She'll scream and cry and lay on the floor kicking her feet like a two year old. She hates doctors. She says all they want to do is poke you and take your money. Other than the eye doctor for her cataracts, she hasn't seen a doctor since my father died. She says they saved him and then ruined his life."

"How long did the hallucination last?"

"Probably only a minute. I'm really worried about her. I hate to burden you with this, Amy."

"Hey, Mom, what are families for?"

"You don't mind hearing this?"

"Of course, I do. Now I'll worry about her. But I want to know what's happening with you two. Always tell me this stuff. Always."

After they got off the phone, Dee thought about Sally Field and her TV family, and wasn't feeling so jealous. A couple minutes later the phone rang and it was Amy again.

"I just talked to Matt, and I'm gonna come home, Mom. If Grandma's hallucinating...then, well, I just want to come see you." She didn't add, before someone drops dead, which Dee guessed was what she was thinking.

"Would it be okay for me to bring Robin? Sam and Walt can stay here and help their dad, but Robin should come with me. Is that good?"

"Yes, yes! I'm so excited. I can't wait to see you."

"It won't be for a couple weeks yet, Mom. I've gotta get plane tickets and take care of some things here first. But soon. Okay."

"I'm very happy, Amy. Thank you."

"Oh, hey, Mom, your birthday's coming up. How about if I aim to be there for your bird-day? Then Robin can sing Hoppy Bird-day to you."

Dee laughed. Amy had always played with words—when she turned sixteen she had spent the day singing, *Hoppy Bird-day to me.*

13. Visitors

"In vain the net is spread in the sight of the bird."
Romanian Proverb

May 2008

When the silver Cadillac pulled up in their driveway on a Saturday afternoon, Dee should have known—Georgie, the big shot, was paying a call. She was surprised, she'd been sure after their lunch date that they wouldn't see him for months or even years.

He wanted something. It must have occurred to Georgie that his ninety-year-old mother could soon be dancing with the angels, so he better hurry to guarantee his due. Georgie wanted his due. Dee knew that their parents' will divided everything equally, so what was his point? What was his hurry?

Dee watched him emerge from his car in an elegant pale gray suit, probably custom made in Italy—Milan, maybe. The passenger door opened and Zita, her brother's perfect wife, climbed out. Dee glanced down at her own sorry fingernails as she watched them approach, and instinctively curled her fingers into her palms, hiding the nails she regularly snacked on. These people were professionally groomed, polished and clipped in all the right places. They could afford to have strangers rub their bodies with heated stones and polish the calluses from their heels. These people gleamed with organic good health.

Georgie opened the back door of the car and lifted out a long white florist's box. Was it filled with wishful thinking stargazer lilies, or maybe long stalks of gladiolas? He was after all, pursuing his inheritance, so funeral flowers would be appropriate. He didn't realize that all Bessie wanted was her son, flowers were extraneous, unnecessary. He didn't need to woo her business or sign her up for a mortgage; all he need do was show up.

Dee watched as he stopped in the driveway and surveyed the property. She could see the curl of his lip, the shake of his head—the place wasn't up to his standards. Well, it wasn't up to her standards either, but it was what she could manage.

Her instinct was to hide, to crunch herself down very small and short, and hide behind the door. *No one's home, go away.* But she ignored her impulses, opened the front door, and welcomed them inside.

Georgie didn't say hello to her; he was obviously on a schedule. "Where's Ma?" he asked. She pointed toward the living room and he marched in—all confidence and power—the handsome, beloved son bearing flowers in a long white box.

Zita gave Dee a quick hug—an arms length motion that avoided coming into contact with any cooties—and blew a kiss that sailed past Dee's cheek without landing. Zita had a perfect skullcap of raven black hair that had no idea that it was over sixty-years-old. Her face was a canvas that had been stretched and tacked into a youthful expression of giddy awe. She was a tiny woman on six-inch heels, whose only career was a war with aging, which she'd been waging since she turned thirty–five and had her first plastic surgery. Boobs, that time.

The two women arrived in the living room in time to see Georgie bend low to kiss Bessie's cheek and place the flower box on her lap.

"What's this?" Bessie said, and Dee watched her mother reach up her hands to caress Georgie's face.

"Open it, Ma. It's flowers for you," Georgie said.

"Oh, Georgie, you didn't have to go and buy me flowers."

"Open the box, Ma." His tone was impatient: *Hop hop, step to it, let's get this show on the road, I don't have all day.*

Bessie, with her twisted arthritic fingers on the box's edge, fumbled, struggled, so Georgie opened it for her. A dozen yellow roses laid in repose inside green florist's tissue.

"Oh, Georgie," Bessie said. "How did you know yellow roses are my favorite?"

"Yes, Georgie, how did you know that?" Dee asked.

"I've always known," he lied.

Bessie was practically swooning.

"But, Georgie, you shouldn't waste your money on me."

"Anything that makes you happy is no waste, Ma." he said.

He looked at Dee, said, "Can you put these in a vase for her, and fix us some coffee?" It was questionable whether the words he said were a question. It was more like your boss telling you to do something, not asking. No please or thank you, and no use of her name. She thought about saying, *do it yourself,* but then didn't want him messing around in the kitchen, or tut-tutting over vegetables with red reduced stickers from grocery store carts of marked-down produce. Dee lifted the box from Bessie's lap and carried it to the kitchen with Zita clacking behind on her high-high heels.

"Shall we make a pot of fresh coffee," Zita said, as she examined the carafe that was still more than half-full of the morning's coffee. She didn't wait for Dee's response, but went ahead and dumped it into the kitchen sink. Two hours old—easy to toss for a woman who never fished between couch cushions for dimes.

Dee plopped the roses into a clear glass vase. Zita scowled at her with her face that couldn't frown.

"Now, Dear," Zita said, "you better let me do that. You know those stems should be trimmed at an angle so the flowers can absorb more water, don't you? Where are your kitchen shears?"

Dee gave her sister-in-law the scissors, and went about making a fresh pot of coffee. She considered getting out a tray, and doing it up fancy with the creamer and sugar bowl and china cups, but instead she pulled out two mugs, one of which had been a wonderful gift from Georgie—a white, crazed, cheap pottery promotional handout with red lettering: Ellison Mortgage. He could drink from his own cheesy cup. She found a second old mug that said, "I love Mom," that made her smile thinking of using that one for Zita, but decided that was being pretty mean spirited, so instead selected a plain blue mug for her sister-in-law. Georgie had wanted a son. Zita had wanted a perfect body.

"You don't have any little treats or anything to go along with the coffee?" Zita asked. "Shall I check the cupboards?"

"I didn't think you ate sweets?" Dee said.

"Oh, my dear, yes, you're right. You know I do watch what I eat, but your brother likes a sweet now and then."

So Dee pulled a package of cookies—vanilla wafers that Bessie loved—from the cupboard and quickly put them on a plate before Zita could notice that the box was dented and had a red reduced sticker. Not quick enough, though.

"Oh, let's just forget the cookies," Zita said. "Your brother doesn't care for stale food."

"Oh well," Dee said, and shrugged, as she popped a whole cookie into her mouth.

"You know, Dee," Zita said, "George thinks you're taking advantage of Bessie. You've been living here rent free for how long now?"

Dee tried not to choke on the cookie.

"Rent free?" She could feel anger screaming up inside of her. "Rent free. When my father couldn't work, who do you think paid the mortgage? Who do you think has been paying all the bills around here?"

"But your father was wealthy. He must have left funds when he died. Surely."

"Well, he didn't."

"They probably went though all their savings when they were taking care of you after the accident."

"Zita, my car insurance and my disability insurance paid for me. My father was a wonderful man, but he liked country clubs and golf and expensive cars. He loved taking his clients out to fancy dinners, impressing people. He lived way beyond his means. There was nothing left when he couldn't work anymore. He never saved. He spent. He even took out a second mortgage on the house. That was just a year before he got sick. And guess who paid it off? Me!"

She was steaming. *So Georgie thinks I'm a mooch.* Her sister-in-law was looking stunned, or puzzled, or occupied calculating dollars and years in her head. Her eyes weren't seeing and she seemed to be without further words, so Dee turned away from her and carried the two cups of coffee to the living room. Zita followed with the impeccable arrangement of yellow roses, each stem clipped at a perfect water-sucking angle.

As Dee entered the living room she saw her mother writing on a blank sheet of paper.

"What're you doing?" she asked.

Bessie looked up from her writing, and said, "Georgie was telling me how beautiful my handwriting is, and he wanted me to write out my name for him, just so's he could look at it every now and then, and be reminded of me. Isn't that precious, Dee?"

Dee stood there a moment, gathering her thoughts. Bessie finished the signature and handed it to her loving son. Georgie, who should've looked guilty, shot an irritated look at Zita. Dee read their faces. Him: *You were supposed to stall her in the kitchen!* Her: *I tried! I tried!* He glanced down at the paper in his lap, he hadn't had time to fold it and stash it in his suit jacket.

Dee had never been known for her gracefulness, never took ballet lessons, and especially since the car accident was somewhat klutzy, so when Georgie reached one hand up for the coffee and she (maybe, or maybe not) thought he had a grip on the cup, but he didn't, the cup with her brother's mortgage company logo fell into his lap and drenched the paper with Bessie's signature. Everyone was shocked and jolted back, when the full cup—all creamed and sugared up and steamy hot—landed on the crotch of his pale gray suit pants, and, oh what a shame, ruined his memento of his mother's signature.

Dee went to get a rag to mop up Georgie's slacks. When she came back into the living room he was still screaming loud profanities at her with Bessie commenting on such ugly talk, reminding him that it was an accident and telling him to take off his pants so she could see if he was burnt, and maybe they should get some butter to put on his, you know, his man parts.

Dee handed him the rag and said, "No, Bessie, not butter, cold water. Ice."

Georgie and Zita didn't stay long after that, even though apologies rushed from Dee's lips, "But really, I'm so sorry. I thought you had hold of it, Georgie. I could bring you a fresh cup of coffee? No? Well, I'm very sorry. Oh, you have to go? I'm so sorry."

The sheet of paper with Bessie's signature was left on the coffee table in a soggy wad, forgotten, not all that useful anymore.

At the front door she watched as their visitors walked away from the house. Birds were singing and gliding around the yard like brown paper airplanes. Zita's heels clacked on the sidewalk. The backside of Georgie's pants was stained brown. It looked like her baby brother had a bad accident, intestinal problems most likely. When he got to the car he stood with the door opened, staring at the creamy leather seat where he'd have to put his soggy brown butt. He grumbled something at Zita, and she scurried around to the car's trunk and brought him a plaid stadium blanket that he placed on the driver's seat. He stood glaring back at Dee standing on the front porch with Bessie. Bessie put up her hand and blew him a kiss. He stared back, looking cross, not blowing back his mother's kiss.

Just before he started to ease himself into the car, a sparrow swooped over him and ejected a white splat that hit Georgie in the forehead and dripped down his face.

The bird had had the last word that day, but Dee knew her brother, and this was only the beginning. Georgie wanted what he wanted and he was used to getting exactly that.

*

But not quite...

Georgie had bragged from the time he was fourteen that he would be going to Harvard or the University of Michigan after high school. He was going to get the best education his parents could buy. He didn't take into consideration that you had to have good grades to do that. He was rejected. He was also rejected by Michigan State, Wayne State, Central Michigan and Western Michigan. No one wanted Georgie.

When Dee had completed three years at MSU, and was back living in Detroit in a tiny, one room apartment down by Wayne State University and going to art school; Georgie was in his senior year of high school and in the throes of rejection letters. All his friends were going away to college.

One Saturday she'd come home for a family dinner, and Georgie had gotten one more rejection letter.

Jack—who over the years had nagged, bribed, scolded and shouted at Georgie to buckle down at school and quit horsing around—had given up.

"Well, maybe you could get a paper route," Jack said, at dinner that night.

Georgie left the table in a rage. Stamping. Screaming. Slamming doors. He left the house in the red car his parents bought him. His tires screeched out of the neighborhood.

Jack said, "He's not stupid. Lazy. Expects life to be handed to him on a silver platter. Maybe his brains got rattled playing football. Too bad he wasn't better at it, if he was any good at it, they'd let him into the good schools. But he didn't even work at that. He spends too much time chasing girls and partying."

"Community college," Dee said. "He could get into community college."

"Army," Jack said.

"Not Army!" Bessie shouted. She got up from the table and started clearing plates not seeming to care that her face was frowning. She stayed in the kitchen, not wanting to listen to Jack talk about the war.

"If he's not in school, he'll be drafted. He'll end up in Vietnam and step on some damn punji stick." Jack said. "He could be drafted anyway, school or not."

And the Army did beckon him. In Georgie's whole life, up until the army took a good look at him, no one had ever noticed the absence of arches on his feet—arches work like shock absorbers and enable a young man to run or jump with the extra weight of packs on his back. Funny, he was able to play football? But, Georgie lucked out and Uncle Sam didn't want him either and never asked him to go to Vietnam.

So Georgie spent, much to his embarrassment, two years at the community college: he buckled down, got a job at a bank in the mortgage department, knocked up Zita (or so everyone mistakenly thought at the time), married her, and eventually opened his own mortgage company.

14. Drip. Drip. Drip

"Some birds avoid water, ducks look for it."
Namibian Proverb

Dee was in a black dark room lying on a hard board. Shadows of men—chanting in a language she didn't understand, sounding gleeful and evil—hovered around the edges of her cell. Their heads were wrapped in red and white checked tablecloths, surprisingly visible in the dark room. They mumbled, laughed and chanted. Guns were firing outside. A man with a long messy beard and amused eyes stood over her head and dripped water onto her face. Drip on her forehead. Drip on her eye. Drip on her nose. This wasn't waterboarding, she thought, or they'd be tilting the board back and pouring water down her nose bringing her near drowning. It *was* retaliation for torture at the CIA's black sites. And then in her dream Dee realized that it wasn't herself about to be waterboarded, it was her son. She startled awake. She hadn't heard anything from Paul in weeks. They had him! He was a prisoner of war in Afghanistan. They were water-boarding him.

Revenge. What did it accomplish? Revenge for three thousand lives lost on 9/11 meant thousands more lives lost in Afghanistan and Iraq, ours and theirs. Water-boarding prisoners by us would mean waterboarding by them. Paul could be a target. She hadn't heard from him.

Drip.

A drop of water landed on her forehead. Thunder and lightning were engaged in a sky war. The roof was leaking.

She wished Sy were still alive. He'd jump out of bed and run for a bucket. With all her energy she shoved her bed to the other side of the room. Sy wasn't alive, so she got a bucket. When she came back into her room she looked up at a drab circle of wet on the ceiling. She put the bucket under the drip.

Now what? They'd needed a new roof for years, it looked bad, but she ignored it. The asbestos shingles had once been black, but all the little bits and bumps of asbestos had worn off from years of snow and sun and wind. Black gone gray—aging like a person.

She had savings, but the money was for a rainy day. On a rainy day she could fly away. Hawaii? It was far away. A place she could fly to, high above everything. And then she could zipline high above the ground, she could ride in a helicopter over the tropical landscape and see down inside a volcano. The beaches would be wonderful too. She imagined herself dressed in clamdigger pants and a huge straw sun hat, walking on a beach collecting seashells.

She'd been saving for a rainy day. Saving up to be able to fly. But this *was* an actual rainy day, or more exactly, 4:00 a.m. on a dark and stormy night.

Her pillow was wet and some of her mattress. They would dry in a day or two, and in the meantime, she'd sleep somewhere else in the house. She sat on the dry part of her mattress and tried to figure out what to do about the roof. She stared at the ceiling while listening to the water hitting the bucket. It was hypnotic—look up, watch a drip gather itself together and then fall into the bucket with a plunk that was almost musical.

Water, water, everywhere, but not a drop to drink.

Where did that come from? She should look it up. She thought of people in New Orleans after the levies broke, and felt blessed. It was only a drip.

She roamed the house, checking all the other rooms for leaks. Bessie was snoring, so she'd wait until morning to check her room. She didn't want her mother to lose sleep and be Mrs. Crabapple.

Wouldn't you know—so far, hers was the only wet room.

But last, she looked into Georgie's old room. It once smelled of dirty socks, stinky feet, or ripe armpits—now it just smelled of dust. It wasn't a room she cleaned or even looked into. Years ago, so long ago that her father was still thriving and healthy, Jack had asked Georgie what he wanted done with his stuff: his high school mementos, the stuffed alligator, model airplanes, and the erector set. It was all still there—a time capsule encased in dust. Why had he left it? Was he locking down his place in the family domain? Her parents had turned her room into a guest room. Georgie's was left as a shrine to his youth, or perhaps, when he didn't clear out his things, they just shut the door and walked away.

She heard a plunk sound and looked up. She'd need another bucket.

*

Dee was sixteen going on her first date—a Saturday night date to the movies. She had spent the day with her hair in rollers. She had shaved her legs, plucked her eyebrows, polished her nails, put on lipstick and a delicate whisk of blush on her cheeks. It was almost time for her double date. Dee was shy in school, but she had friends, her not-gorgeous Eleanor Roosevelt face wasn't threatening to other girls or intimidating to boys.

She was ready—feeling good about herself, feeling pretty. She had come out of her room and was walking down the hall, when Georgie came out of his room behind her.

"Hey, Dee," he called, "look at this!"

She turned and that's when he shot her in the face with a squirt gun.

That night she told her friends about the shooting, her best friend Kim had been indignant and said Georgie was a monster. But the boys laughed and said that they wished they'd seen her face. Then she laughed too, because that was what you did then—when the boys laughed you laughed too.

*

After all these years and all the happiness she'd had in her life (forget the pain), water in the face didn't matter much. Except that she worried about her son, Paul—and the Taliban and Al Qaeda. And floods after the Arctic ice caps melted. Water, water everywhere, but not a drop to drink.

To stop worrying, she went to her computer and found the poem. It was *The Rime of the Ancient Mariner* by Samuel Taylor Coleridge, 1772-1834, and the original rhyme was:

> *Water, water, everywhere*
> *And all the boards did shrink;*
> *Water, water, everywhere,*
> *Nor any drop to drink,*

Dee printed a copy of the long poem and took it into the kitchen and made coffee. She sat at the table and read over the poem several times, listening to the rain hit the windows, until at last the rain stopped and morning arrived dressed in a coral pink glow.

Bessie came into the kitchen, having sat her way down the stairs one butt thump at a time. The "up" version was Bessie climbing on all fours like a very large dog, a Great Dane maybe, with Dee following to catch her if necessary, which would probably kill them both.

Dee said, "The silly buckets on the deck, that had so long remained, I dreamt that they were filled with dew. And when I awoke, it rained."

Bessie, looking perplexed, asked, "Is that a poem?"

Dee nodded.

"The roof's leaking."

*

Dee's plan was pretty farfetched, but she had nothing to lose. Should she be meek and whining, or should she be strong and firm—a powerhouse? Which would work better? She called Georgie's cell phone. They hadn't spoken since the missed connection of the coffee cup she dropped or he didn't grab.

When he answered on the second ring and heard her voice, he said, "What? Has something happened to Ma?"

"Bessie's fine." She hesitated. "But I'm not fine."

"Listen, Dee, if you're sick, I'm sorry. Call a doctor. I'm busy."

It was nine o'clock on Sunday morning. He sounded like he'd been awake for hours, she heard men talking in the background and distant birds. An early round of golf? Probably.

"You've been wanting your share, Georgie. Well, I think it's time for you to get your share."

Silence.

Then a confused sounding Georgie said, "Huh? What did you say?"

"Yes, Georgie," she said sweetly. "Your mother's house needs a new roof, and it only seems fair for you to take care of it."

"Why the hell would I do that? You live there. You take care of it."

Dee got her voice all sugared up into a diabetic nightmare, "Why you should do it, is because all your mother has coming in is Dad's social security and mine. There're no funds, and you're her son with the Rolex."

"Like I said," Georgie sounded irritated, put-upon. "Like I said, it's not my problem. You deal with it."

She wanted to say, "Your cheesy lawyer tried to sue for your share of the estate. Ginger, your girl, was sneaking around in Dad's files, and then you come over trying to get Bessie's signature. You want your due, by hook or by crook." But she didn't.

"Here's the thing," she said. "I know you're looking forward to getting your share of the estate. But if the roof falls in, or if the whole house is water damaged, the estate won't be worth much. And when, because of the moisture, black mold grows all over everything and your mother and I die from black moldy lungs and you get the house, but it's worthless and has to be torn down, then all you'll get is the land it sits on. Think of it as protecting your investment. And, George, one other very important thing." she stopped speaking.

"Yeah, what?"

"Your mother, the woman who loves you more than anything, lives here."

And then she hung up.

*

On Tuesday, after Dee emptied the buckets of rainwater and fixed Bessie's lunch, Georgie's response to her request for help with the leaking roof came in the mail. It was a bill for $3,500 to replace his coffee ruined suit.

Dee said, "Damn him."

Bessie said, "Now, Dee, you know I don't like that kind of ugly talk."

Dee handed her mother George's handwritten note. In big red letters he wrote, "YOU OWE ME!!!"

"What happened to Georgie's suit?" Bessie asked.

"Remember the day he brought you the flowers, the yellow roses, and he didn't get hold of his coffee cup and it spilled on his suit. He wants me to pay for it."

"But, Dee, that was an accident." Bessie shook her head. "$3,500 for a suit, that's awfully expensive. Why, I think we bought our first Lincoln for a way less than that."

"He's mad because I asked him to help us pay for a new roof."

Bessie pinched her lips together for several seconds before saying, "Dee, now you know he shouldn't have to spend his hard-earned money on our roof. We can buy our own roof."

"We?" Dee asked. "Do you have a secret stash that I don't know about, Bessie?"

"Now, Dee, you know that your father's a good provider. He can pay for a roof, surely."

"Bessie, Jack's been dead for years."

Bessie looked huffy, punched her fists into her hips and said, "I know that! I'm not going senile. Just so's you know, Dee, I maybe forget some things sometimes, but I'm not stupid."

"Dad left us a huge debt that I paid off. He took out a second mortgage, and then couldn't work any more. Did you know that, Bessie? I still have some savings and I guess there's no choice. I'll be paying for the roof."

She thought of luaus and hula dancers and Mai Tais in Hawaii, and flying, flying, flying, and wanted to cry. A roof wasn't any fun. There was no dream quotient to a roof, other than not dreaming you're being waterboarded.

Georgie wouldn't show up, in fact, she knew they wouldn't be hearing from him for a while and in some ways she was relieved. If he paid for the roof, he'd feel entitled, but then he already felt entitled. She would pay for the roof. The trip to Hawaii would morph into a roof over her and Bessie's heads.

"I can help you pay for the roof, Dee," Bessie said, in almost a whisper.

Dee smiled at Bessie, and got up from her chair and kissed Bessie on the forehead.

"Bessie, thank you. But you don't have any money."

"But, Dee. Remember when you got married, and I told you what my mother told me. A woman should always have a secret bit of money put away, just so's if her husband leaves her, or he's a bad man, or anything like that, just so's she can keep herself safe. Did you not do that? Did you not keep a little secret stash, like I told you?"

"I thought you meant a ten dollar bill hidden in the back of your wallet. And yes, I do that. But it won't pay for a roof."

Bessie said, "I wish my brother Rob was still living. Maybe he'd loan us money for the roof. I feel lonely, Dee."

"I know, Bessie. I know." Dee said. "Well, you have me. And remember Amy and Robin are coming next week. They'll be here for my birthday. You have people, Bessie."

"I don't know a Robin."

"Robin's my granddaughter, she's four. She was a late baby. Her brothers are in junior high school. We haven't seen Robin since she was just a year old. She's your great-granddaughter."

"They could stay in Georgie's old bedroom," Bessie said. "He never sleeps here anymore. We should probably clean it."

"Yeah, we should. The ceiling was leaking in there too."

Bessie, sighed, so loud and deep, Dee wasn't sure if it was theatrics, or if she was in some physical pain.

"We should go to the bank," Bessie said, almost like she was talking about going to a loved one's funeral. "We have to take care of business."

15. BANKING

"He sells the bird on the branch."
Italian Proverb

After Bessie spent an hour searching for her savings passbook, they drove to the bank. She had it clutched in her hand—a passbook ancient and frayed, its blue cover crackled and dry, filled with Bessie's tiny writing. Dee had never seen it before.

"Your father never knew about my savings."

At the bank, Bessie snailed her way up to the teller, using her black cane more than usual, her normally perfect posture was suddenly bent, and Dee knew it was all for affect, so that the bankers would give the little old lady special attention.

Dee stood behind her mother as Bessie handed the passbook to the teller. The Chase Bank teller took the NBD bank savings passbook and stared at it like it was a petrified hunk of tree from the dark ages.

"What is this?" she said.

"It's my savings," Bessie said, in her most intentionally quivering old lady voice.

"But, Mam..." the teller looked around, desperate to give this weird senior citizen away. Her eyes locked on someone across the lobby and she raised her hand, a beacon of distress. A few moments later a suited man came up and asked what the problem was and the teller handed him the NBD passbook.

"Oh," he said, and then smiled at Bessie and Dee. He introduced himself, but Dee didn't pay attention to his name. He was the manager, and that was the important part. "Please come with me," he said.

In his cubicle he directed them to the two chairs across from his desk, and they all sat. He examined the passbook.

"National Bank of Detroit." He turned the booklet over in his hand, opened it. "Back a good number of years ago, in the nineties, it was, NBD merged with First One of Chicago and became Bank One. The bank was purchased by J.P. Morgan Chase two years ago, in 2006. Heck, Miss Ellison, I'm sorry, but I can't really help you with this."

"So, are you telling me that my savings are no good?" Bessie said.

"Oh, no, no, Miss Ellison," he said, all the while smiling with very straight white teeth. "Your savings are good, it's just that we don't have your account here. The account would be considered abandoned since there's been no activity for so many years." He looked at the last entry. "Twenty-two years." He had the syrup dripping smile young businessmen use for little old ladies. "We have to send abandoned accounts to the State. Legally we can't collect interest on them. You'll have to go on line to the State of Michigan website. They have forms there for you to fill out."

They drove home without saying much.

"I don't know how to go online, Dee. The only lines I know how to go on are clotheslines."

Dee laughed, and asked, "So when was the last time you touched a clothesline?"

"Well, just so's you know, I quit hanging clothes out because of the darn birds thinking that my sheets were their...you know what."

"Outhouse? Bathroom? Privy?" Dee asked. She didn't mention that she had been doing the laundry for years, ever since her father had gotten sick.

"I know about telephone lines," Bessie said.

"Now you're bragging."

"I don't know how to do any of that computer stuff. Why is everything having to be done on computers now?"

"I'll do it, Bessie, I can do it. How much was in that account, anyway?"

Bessie fumbled the passbook out of her purse and peered at the last entry.

"One hundred, twenty-seven dollars and fifty nine cents."

Groceries. A utility bill. No roof. Dee wished she had asked that stupid, most important question before they ventured out. She would go on line and find her mother's abandoned account, and meantime they'd make Georgie's room presentable for company, Amy and Robin would be coming in just a few days.

16. ON BEING A CUSHION

"Two birds disputed about a kernel,
when a third swooped down and carried it off."
African Proverb

On cleaning day Dee followed Bessie up the stairs, in case she had to catch her or break her fall with her own body, crappy job being a cushion for someone else's fall.

"It's a chore climbing those stairs, Dee," Bessie said, after she caught her breath at the top. "Maybe we should be living in a one story house or apartment?"

"But, Bessie," Dee said, "maybe climbing the stairs is what keeps us healthy, besides you love this house, don't you?" Dee wasn't in love with the house. A first floor apartment would be much easier, less to clean, no lawn to feel guilty about. Easier. But the hard part would be clearing this house out, preparing it for sale. Just thinking about it was overwhelming.

"I'm thinking that it's too much for you to manage, Dee. You're looking really old."

"I'm not the only one."

"Hmph," Bessie said. "And your birthday's coming. Then you're going to be even older."

"You're only as old as you feel, Bessie." Dee called out, as she went back down the stairs to get the heavy Hoover.

"Well then, I'm very, very old." Bessie shouted down to her. "Sometimes, I just think I've been living too long. I get tired. Just so's you know, Dee, I wouldn't be sad to be done with it all. I've had a pretty good life. There's not a lot to look forward to."

"Robin and Amy are coming to visit." Dee said, as she reached the top step.

No reaction from Bessie.

Dee said. "Well, after they're gone, we could go to Costco and have some snacks."

"Okay, then. After that, then I'll be ready to cross over to the pearly gates."

"You sure that's the direction you'll be going?"

"Ha!" Bessie said, and grinning, wagged her bent arthritic finger at Dee, then wagged it skyward, "I know where I'm goin', but where are you going?"

"I'm going to clean Georgie's room."

"Seriously, Dee, I'm ready to go...anytime, just so's you know. I've had a long good life. Enough is enough already. Don't you let anyone hook me up to any breathing machine or anything like that, okay?"

"Okay."

As they talked, they walked down the upstairs corridor until they reached Georgie's old bedroom. They stopped and stood together staring into the dim space. The blinds were down, making the dark blue room even darker. When he was in junior high, Georgie and their father had debunked the bunk beds, arranging the two twin beds against opposite walls with his desk between.

Dee felt overwhelmed and tired just looking into the room, or maybe it was the two trips up and down the stairs that wore her out. "We could just dust and put fresh bedding on the beds?" Dee suggested. "And vacuum. Huh? Well, that sounds like we'll be doing it all."

Bessie sat on the desk chair while Dee dusted and changed the beds. She—very helpfully—lifted her feet so Dee could vacuum under them.

There was a fourth bedroom that they might have used for their company, but it had no bed, just Bessie's old Singer sewing machine, an aged dress form, a chest stuffed with fabric scraps, and a flower-patterned upholstered chaise, that Dee had slept on until her own bed dried out.

Bessie was fingering white marbles in an old soup bowl.

She said, "Remember how Georgie carried marbles wherever he went, Dee?"

Dee stopped dusting and came to look.

"Yes, of course, I remember how lumpy Georgie's pockets were whenever he left the house. He said he carried the marbles for safety, that if anyone tried to kidnap him he'd leave a trail of marbles, so he could be found. Birds would eat breadcrumbs, if he used them, then his trail would be in some sparrow's belly, and he'd be doomed. Marbles were better, except that they rolled."

Dee remembered how Bessie was afraid that someone might abscond with her beautiful boy. She had been a young teen during the Lindbergh kidnapping in 1932, and she talked about it all the time when they were growing up, or anyway, it seemed like she did. She had Georgie convinced that any day, at any time, someone would leap out of an alley and grab him, even though there were no alleys in their neighborhood.

Dee held a few marbles in her hand, rolling them around in her palm, and wondered at the fact that she was never afraid of being kidnapped. Instead, she worried about being deserted, left behind. When she was little, Dee believed her mother was trying to lose her, Bessie moved at a pace faster than a small child's legs could run. Bessie walked fast—always, before Georgie arrived in their lives and after—whether up the street pushing the baby buggy, or through the stores, it was almost as though she were in some marathon, and Dee had to run to keep up. Racing, always racing, trying not to be left behind, then Bessie would suddenly stop to look at something, or to adjust Georgie's blanket in the buggy, and Dee would slam into her, which irritated Bessie and she'd snap, "Stay off my heels, Dee. You're always runnin' into me."

How different their lives had been, living in the same house with the same parents, one was valuable and one was not.

Dee wanted to get a big black garbage bag and put all of Georgie's stuff out for the trash. "Can't we just throw all this stuff out, Bessie? Or donate it?"

"But, Dee," Bessie said, "it's not ours. What if Georgie wants it someday."

"Bessie, he's sixty," she paused a second, calculating. "Sixty-one. I would think that if he wanted this stuff, he'd have gotten it by now."

"I had a beautiful doll, a Madame Alexander. Is that right, Dee? Madame Alexander? I had it when I was growing up. I wish I still had it. She had blond hair, like I did, and a filmy long pink evening gown. So, no, I don't want us to get rid of Georgie's things. I still want my old toys, even at this age. Just to hold them."

Was Bessie remembering her own doll, or the one that Dee got for Christmas when she was ten? She could still picture her first sight of the beautiful doll dressed in a long pink gown made of sheer chiffon over satin, sitting on the piano bench, facing the keys of the baby grand piano on Christmas morning. Her father had picked it out, had actually gone to a toy store and bought it for her, which made it especially precious. A few years later, Georgie had gone into her room and had taken the doll from her shelf. He snapped off her head, and flushed it down the toilet. The yellow hair went down the drain, but the doll's head got stuck. The plumber had to come. Dee was older by then, maybe twelve or thirteen, but she cried. Her brother murdered her favorite doll. He never touched or hurt any of her other dolls, so he wasn't a serial killer. He just chose the prettiest, the one with her dress perfectly arranged on a messy shelf, the one she loved the most—the one her father gave her.

17. FOUR GENERATIONS

"Flying birds have no master."
French Proverb

Dee paced. What she really wanted was a cigarette. A whole one. Or maybe just one deep long drag would be enough. But a week ago she had decided that she didn't want her little granddaughter to see her bad habit, so she quit. Just like that. She decided that it was a bad thing and simply stopped. Cold turkey, or considering the fact that she had been down to only one cigarette a day, you could probably call it cold hummingbird.

Soon. Amy and Robin would be arriving at the house soon. The plane that brought them from Milwaukee to Detroit had landed at Metropolitan Airport. Amy called while waiting in a long line for a rental car. Dee was pacing, going from the window in the dining room to the living room window, where she carefully pulled back the edge of the aged brittle window shade to peek out at the street. They were on their way, but the minutes ticked by too slowly for Dee.

"Just so's you know, Dee, you're wearing out the carpet."

Finally, just in time for the sake of the Oriental rug, a black car pulled into the driveway, and Amy got out. Dee and Bessie went out on the front porch. Amy waved, then opened the car's back door and fiddled around with seatbelts. Suddenly, like a cork popping out of a champagne bottle, a small girl with long blond hair burst out of a car seat and came running up the front porch steps.

"You're my two grandma's," she informed them. "My great grandma and my just grandma-grandma."

Dee squatted down and put out her arms. "Can I hug you?"

"Certainly!" Robin said and squealed as Dee kissed her neck during the hug. Ticklish. Sy had been very ticklish, his feet, his armpits, his belly, his groin, his knees. She missed her ticklish husband. Ticklish—a sign of life. Sy hadn't been ticklish in a very long time.

Bessie stood leaning on her black cane, and Robin said, "I like your stick," and hugged Bessie around her knees. Bessie patted the little blond head and looked happy. "Mommy said I should call you Bessie. We don't want to get confused with too many grandma's around here."

Bessie had insisted on being called Bessie when Amy was tiny. She said that she didn't want anyone to think she was old enough to be a grandmother.

"Mom, mommy," Robin called out to Amy, who was pulling a suitcase and backpack out of the trunk. "Hurry up, and come get some hugs." Then she raced down to the car and took a pink backpack from her mother. By the way she trudged with it, Dee thought it must contain a few bricks.

Amy hugged Dee and then kissed her cheek.

"Hi, Mom," she said.

Robin said, "Hey, that's not 'mom'. That's grandma. You're mom."

"But, Robin, your grandma is my mom. And your great grandma," she turned then and hugged Bessie, "is my grandmother."

"It's very confusing," Robin said. "Everyone is a mother and a grandmother at the same time."

*

Bessie stayed downstairs in the kitchen while Dee took Amy and Robin to Georgie's blue room where they'd sleep.

"How's Bessie doing?" Amy asked in a hushed tone.

"She's been amazingly good," Dee said, also hushed. "She suggested that we should move to a one story place. She hasn't seen any dogs in the house since I talked to you on the phone that night. It's like it was a blip on a radar screen, there, then gone. And she hasn't wandered off again. "

"Grandma," Robin said, and tugged on Dee's pant leg. "Grandma, is this bucket of water here for me to play with. I can't take a bath in it, because I'm too big."

"Oh, no, Sweetie, the roof's been leaking. That bucket is to catch drips until I can get the roof fixed."

Robin's attention had flitted on to Georgie's toys in the room.

"Can I play with these marbles?"

"Yes," Dee said.

"Robin," Amy said, "I think you should just play with them in the bowl, someone could slip on them if they're rolling around on the floor. We don't want anyone to get hurt, right?"

"Right!" Robin said. "We have to be good, because old people live here. Old people are fragile. Right, Grandma?"

But before Dee could answer, Robin bounced away from the marbles because she noticed the stuffed alligator. She hugged the toy and a cloud of dust rose around her.

"Oh, Geez," Dee said, "I think that alligator needs a bath. Do you want to help me get him washed up?"

"Yes." Robin started jiggling happily. "Do we give him a bath in the bathtub with me?"

"She loves baths," Amy said. "Can you tell?"

"He's really dirty," Dee said. "Maybe we should wash him in the washing machine. He'd make your bathwater icky."

"Does your washing machine have a TV screen so we can watch him jumping around in the bubbles?"

"Yes." A front loader with a window, who'd of guessed that a washing machine could be a source of entertainment for a four-year-old.

"Okay, then let's wash him. What's his name anyway? Can I name him? What's a good name, Grandma? Is it a boy alligator or a girl alligator?"

"Maybe we should wait a while, Robin," Amy said. "We just got here and we want to visit with Bessie too."

"Grandma, I have a bunny. Do you want to see her? She's very, very, very soft." Robin said, as she was digging into her backpack tossing irrelevant objects, like clothes, on the bed. "Her name is Fluffy. You know why, Grandma? Cause she's so very, very, very fluffy and soft. She likes to sleep with me." She held a stuffed bunny up to Dee. "You can hold her. Put her by your cheek."

Dee put the little bunny against her cheek and closed her eyes, smiled. "Ahh, so soft. Why, Robin, this is the softest bunny I've ever felt."

Robin looked pleased. "Told ya," she said.

Dee left Amy and Robin to finish unpacking and settle in. Downstairs she found Bessie sitting at the kitchen table looking sullen.

"What's wrong?"

"Nothing."

"Bessie?"

"What?"

"Why are you looking pissy?"

"I'm not looking like that, and you know I don't like that kind of ugly talk."

"Okay then," Dee said, and walked away to set up a fresh pot of coffee. "Would you like a cup of coffee?"

"I thought you forgot about me," Bessie said.

"I didn't forget about you, I was just helping them get settled in their room."

"I was lonely. I heard laughing."

Bessie was as emotionally fragile as her thin skin, which looked like easily torn tissue paper, transparent, revealing all the workings, the blue veins and prominent bones, beneath.

"I'm sorry," Dee said. "Next time, you should come upstairs with us. Okay?"

They had been together for years, the past ten, after her father died, it had been just her and Bessie. Of course, Bessie was jealous. She wasn't used to sharing. Dee decided that she'd have to be careful to include her mother in whatever they did over the next few days.

But, if she were given a lie detector test at that moment, she'd have to admit that she resented it, somewhat, or maybe a lot. She wanted to spend every second with Amy and Robin. She was, truth here, or the little line drawn on the lie detector would jump up, sick of Bessie. She was sick of catering to her, sick of having her world revolve around what Bessie wanted, liked, or disapproved of. She wanted to swear with gusto, she wanted to say every word that Bessie didn't like her sanctimonious ears to hear. She wanted to shout, "PISSY!" as loud as she could.

When Amy came into the kitchen, followed by Robin carrying the very soft bunny in one hand and the dirty alligator in the other, Dee said, "Robin, do you want to let Bessie feel how soft Fluffy is?"

"Certainly!" Robin shouted. "Put her by your cheek." She handed Bessie the bunny and waited, watching intently for Bessie's reaction.

Please, say something good, be kind, be gentle, think of the child first, Dee silently prayed to her mother.

Bessie, rubbed the bunny on her cheek, then said sweetly, "Very soft," and handed the bunny back.

Robin looked satisfied, then tugged at Dee's pant leg, "Can we watch washing machine TV now, Grandma? We gotta get this alligator cleaned up, right?"

"Bessie, do you want to come down the basement with us?" Dee said. She would have preferred to scream, "Pissy," but was, as usual, a good person.

Bessie looked torn. She didn't want to be left out, but she also looked like she didn't relish making the stair trip.

Amy said, "Bessie, why don't you and I just sit and chat, I haven't seen you in so long."

Dee puckered a little kiss in her daughter's direction and went down the basement without Bessie.

18. HAVING WINGS

"A butterfly thinks itself a bird because it can fly."
African Proverb

There are so many places to explore when you're four: basements and attics and backyards. There are stories to hear, to take in with your growing brain sopping in facts and fanciful ideas, and then storing them in the nooks and crannies inside your head. Dee observed her granddaughter's hunger to know, and was struck by the difference between Robin's young brain and Bessie's old one. Thinking of her own brain, she wondered, what tricks could there be? How much attention and energy would it take to get back that enthusiasm for learning that her four-year-old granddaughter had?

She sat with the child watching the washing machine, Dee on an old kitchen chair, and Robin on an overturned laundry basket. Every time the stuffed alligator appeared in the bubbles, Robin would shout, "There he is! There he is!"

"He doesn't mind getting his face in the water, Grandma," she said, "He's not scared. I can put my face in the water. Did you know that I can swim?"

"Do you get swimming lessons at home?" Dee asked.

"Yes. Daddy teaches me in the lake. I have floaties. Guess what color? Just guess."

"Pink?"

"Yes! Pink. Did you guess that pink was my favorite color?"

"I did."

"I wish you could come to my house, Grandma. I could show you my bedroom."

"Is it pink?"

"Certainly!" Robin shouted, and laughed with delight.

There's a rather cliché idea about being so overwhelmed with love that your heart feels like it's growing, getting big inside your chest, just about to burst—bursting with love. And that was exactly what Dee felt.

"When I was a little girl I had a pink bedroom too."

"Did my mommy have a pink bedroom just like me and you?"

"Hers was purple and lavender. Very pretty."

"I think she still likes purple. She has many purple sweaters," Robin said, then bounced off her perch on the laundry basket and stood beside Dee. "Give me your ear and I'll tell you a secret."

Dee tipped her head to the side, and Robin whispered, "I'm going to have pink sweaters when I'm a mom."

After another minute passed, Robin said, "I'm getting tired of watching washing machine TV. Can we see what else is down here?"

Dee was also getting bored with a TV that just bubbled and thumped.

"There's the coal bin room, very dirty and there's nothing in there. And there's an old workbench." She pointed across the room. "And then there's the big room where all my stuff from my old house is."

"Let's go see it!" Robin shouted and tugged Dee's arm.

The big room took up half the basement and was stacked with cardboard boxes and furniture piled up to the ceiling.

"I forgot how much stuff there was in here," Dee said.

As they explored she felt a pulling in her chest—Sy's recliner, he'd been gone so long it should be easy to look at. Should be. Wasn't. If it had been in sight all the time, would she have ever started seeing it as just a comfortable place to sit? The red leather Lips sofa that Sy bought her for their anniversary was covered with a sheet. She pulled the covering off, and Robin squealed with joy. She stretched out on it and then kissed it with a fake movie passion. They both laughed.

"I like this kissy couch, Grandma. Why don't you put it upstairs where you can see it everyday."

"You saw how crowded with furniture it is up there. No room."

Bessie's stuff. Her father's stuff. No room for hers. When her house was sold and her life boxed up and put in the basement, she'd still been in rehab, still walking with crutches and unable to decide anything. So it was all here, nothing sorted or tossed, simply boxed up by movers and stored. All her things were in a coma, just sitting here waiting to be kissed awake like Sleeping Beauty. Thankfully the basement was always dry, no mold, no floods, a safe dry place to store her life.

If the accident had never happened, would they still live in Indian Village. Maybe Bessie would have been living in their house, instead of the other way around.

"Okay, Grandma, so now could we check out your yard. Do you have swings?"

"I don't, but we could go see the yard anyway." Dee was happy to leave the basement.

When they came into the kitchen, Bessie looked relaxed and happy, and Dee realized how much she had dreaded seeing Bessie's face. Would she be pouting? But no, happily, Amy was spoon-feeding Bessie's ego.

"We want to go outside and play. Would you two like to come too?" Dee said.

"Whaddaya say, Bessie?" Amy said, "Shall we go outside and play?"

They got Bessie settled in a yellow chair in the backyard, while Robin was dashing around exploring the old vegetable garden and an ancient rose bush that amazingly had a few blooms. She ran over to Dee and asked, "Do you have a ball? I'm a good catcher. Usually."

"Oh dear, I'm sorry, Robin. I don't. I have a little shovel in the garage if you want to dig in the garden."

"Okay," Robin said, and started twirling on the weedy lawn.

In the garage, Dee found the bucket and trowel Bessie had used for weeding a few times since spring. She was surprised that Robin had stayed behind, and didn't join her and explore the garage. When she came out, she didn't see Robin dancing across the yard. Amy and Bessie were standing near the spot where they had found asparagus. Where was Robin?

And then she saw her across the yard climbing over the fence and into the dog run. Robin jumped down on the other side. Dee stood unmoving, staring at the four-year old in the dog run, the same dog run that she had been locked up in when she was four. Robin climbed in and then after looking around, climbed back up the gate, sticking her toes between the chain links. She crouched at the top, and then jumped with her arms flung out, a little bird of a girl taking flight.

Dee stood there, feeling like she was about to cry. When she was four, it never occurred to her that she could climb out of the dog run. She was put there by her mother and she stayed there with the dog she called

Mommy. Robin had wings, and for whatever reason, obedience or timidity, Dee's wings had been clipped or had never developed. She'd never be able to fly.

19. DISTRACTION

"There are no birds in last years nest."
Spanish Proverb

Amy and Robin had been visiting for four days, two of which they spent with Amy's friends that lived in the Metropolitan Detroit area. Dee tried not to be jealous, and smothered her desire for Amy to spend every available minute with her. A part of her wanted to whine and tearfully ask her daughter why on this rare visit she had to see other people. *Why not just spend the time with me?* But she wouldn't do that. She refused to be that person. She'd listened to Bessie whining for Georgie's company. It didn't work. It was off-putting, and had the opposite effect. You're no fun to be with when you waste your time begging for more time. Don't be greedy. Enjoy them like you would a rich dessert. Savor the time you actually get to be with them. Shut up, and let them be free to love you...or not.

She wondered if she herself had moved away and then came back home to visit, whom would she see?

There was no one. The friends she had known—in school, in her old neighborhoods, at work—were all vague memories. She no longer had any friends. There was just Bessie.

Sondra, who had been warm and welcoming when Dee and Sy moved in next door to her in Indian Village, had come to visit when Dee was still hobbling around with a walker after the accident. Bessie had mistaken the black woman ringing the doorbell as a Jehovah's Witness, and she wasn't going to open the door. "But she has flowers and parked in the driveway," Dee said. "Jehovah Witnesses don't bring flowers." Dee, even with her memory blurry, recognized her neighbor and invited her in for coffee. Bessie hovered, worrying that the silverware would disappear, or something not to her liking would happen in her house—a black woman sat at the dining room table. Oh no! And she wasn't even a maid taking a break, and in that case it would have to be in the kitchen.

When Dee and Georgie were kids, Bessie had a "colored" woman named Beulah come in once a week to help with the chores. Dee remembered Beulah's kind manner. She remembered sitting at the kitchen table when she was five or six, while Beulah ate her lunch.

"Do you want to know how my skin came to be brown?" Beulah had asked.

Dee nodded, she never saw people who were darker colors than her.

Beulah leaned in toward Dee and whispered, "It's from drinking coffee."

And that must be true, Dee thought, because Beulah's skin was the same color as the cup of creamed coffee she was drinking. Dee wanted her skin to be that color too, so when Beulah went to the lavatory, she snuck a large gulp of the coffee, then checked her hand. She would need to drink more coffee for her skin to be so pretty.

When Sondra came with flowers, Bessie hovered. Her message was clear—a black person could work for you, but couldn't be your friend. And now a black man was running for president, on June 3, Obama was declared as the presumptive nominee for the Democratic party. Dee and Amy applauded as they watched the news. Bessie left the room.

*

On June 4th, the morning before Dee's birthday four generations of females sat having breakfast around the kitchen table.

"Oh," Amy said, almost like an afterthought, "I'm meeting Laura and her daughter, Megan, for lunch today. Don't worry about watching Robin, Mom. They want to meet her too."

Dee smiled and then said, "Well, that'll be nice. Is Megan Robin's age?"

Chair legs screeched on the kitchen floor as Bessie abruptly got up from the table and left the kitchen. Dee and Amy watched her leave and then frowned at each other.

"Where's she off to?" Amy asked, "Megan's a little older I think. Does Bessie usually leave the table like that?"

"No, maybe she's heading to the bathroom? She never leaves food. In fact, sometimes she picks up her plate and licks it."

"Really!" Robin said, looking impressed and delighted.

"Oops," Dee said.

"I like to lick ice cream bowls." Robin said.

Bessie came back into the kitchen with her winter coat on and her purse under her arm. "I'm ready to go home now," she said.

The three at the table looked at each other and then back at Bessie.

"Bessie, you are home," Amy and Dee said at the same time.

"No, I want to go to *my* home. I live in Traverse City. Will someone please drive me?"

"Bessie, you live here. You've lived here for more than sixty years," Dee said.

Bessie started to cry. "You're lying. You're saying that just so's you don't have to give me a ride home." She sobbed, then shouted, "I want to go home right now!" Then she stamped her foot.

"I'm scared," Robin whispered. "What's happening?"

Dee reached over and touched Robin's shoulder, and whispered, "It'll be okay. Don't be scared. Bessie's just confused."

"Just so's you know, I heard that and I'm not confused. Don't whisper about me." Then she shouted, "I want someone to take me home!"

"Okay, Bessie," Amy said. "I'll drive you home. Just give me a few minutes to change out of my pajamas. Okay?"

Bessie sniffled and nodded.

Amy ran upstairs.

Dee patted Bessie's chair seat. "Bessie, come sit at the table with Robin and me, and tell us why you're so anxious to go home."

Bessie sat.

"Yeah," Robin said with her little forehead wrinkled with worry, "why do you want to go home so bad?"

"I miss my mother," Bessie said and wiped her eyes with a soggy tissue.

"Does she live very far away?" Robin asked.

"Yes. She's far, far away."

"If my mommy was far away, I'd miss her so much. I'd cry too." Robin got up from her chair and hugged Bessie. "My mommy's a very good mommy too. She's a good driver too."

When Amy came back, she jingled the rental car's keys. "Ready, Bessie?"

Dee and Robin stood on the front porch and waved as Amy and Bessie drove off.

"Will they be gone visiting Bessie's mommy for a long time?" Robin asked.

Dee hesitated before responding, concerned about mentioning death to a four-year-old, but couldn't think of a way around it. "No, Robin, Bessie's mother died a long-long time ago."

"Hmm, yeah, I think that Bessie's mother would be so very old. We had a cat that got very old and died. We buried him in our yard and put a stone on top. His name was Gherkin, like a pickle."

"So you understand about people and pets dying."

"Yep, Mom says I'm old for my age. But, Grandma, if Bessie's mommy died, where are they going to go?"

"I think that by taking her for a ride, your mom is trying to get Bessie's mind off going home. Hopefully, she'll forget all about wanting to see her mother."

"It's a trick then?"

"Yep, it's a trick."

"When my mom was babysitting for her friend's little boy one time, he kept crying and wanting his mommy. So she put him into his car seat and drove him around till he fell asleep."

"Did you go too?"

"Certainly!" Robin said, and laughed. "It's a trick. Dis-action."

"Distraction?"

"Yep. That's it. Mom said she pretended to take him home until he forgot that he wanted to go home."

20. HOPPY BIRD-DAY

"Birds of a feather flock together."
English Proverb

Dee was sixty-five years old, old enough for Medicare. She woke up on her birthday feeling like she was being watched. She opened her eyes and Robin was standing at the side of the bed.

"Can I climb in with you, Grandma?"

Dee pushed back the covers and patted the space beside her.

"This is the best birthday present I could ever wish for," she said.

"No, Grandma, we have real presents for you. You will be sooo happy. You will! I promise.

"But I'm sooo happy right now."

"Yeah, but I betcha you'll be even more sooo happy. You get two presents. I helped pick-um. Me and Mom went birthday present shopping when she told you we were going to see her friend. It was a white fib."

And Dee was sooo happy all day. The fact that Bessie pouted because she wasn't the center of attention, or that she hadn't gotten a gift for Dee (How could she?) was obscured by Robin's exuberance. Joy overrode pissy and even Bessie smiled now and then. Amy never left to visit other people. Dee had them all to herself. What more could she want?

Around noon the doorbell rang and Amy ran to answer. She came into the kitchen with a bouquet, an edible arrangement. The card said, "Hoppy Bird-day, Mom. I love you, Paul."

Dee got teary.

"I worry about him all the time," she said. "How could he do this from Afghanistan or Iraq or Pakistan? I don't even know for sure where he is."

"Okay," Amy said. "I confess. He wrote me and asked if I'd order flowers for your birthday. So these are flowers...sort of."

The fact that her children communicated, perhaps Paul was in contact with Amy more than with her, was comforting. They liked each other. Was that rare? Or was that more normal than the way she and Georgie got along?

"Grandma, can I eat a pineapple flower?" Robin said.

"We can all have fruit flowers for lunch," Dee said. She felt an extra lift of her spirits, and realized how there was almost always a little nagging fear, a small pain in the bottom of her gut, a dread for her son. Paul was safe, or at least he was a few days ago. Safe.

*

After their early dinner there was a pretty box with half a dozen very fancy cupcakes with pink icing. Each one was different.

"Which one is the bestest, Grandma?"

"It's so hard to choose. Which do you think, Robin?"

Robin contemplated for a minute, then pointed.

"Okay," Dee said, "I want that one."

Amy took it from the box, set it in front of Dee and put a candle in its center.

When it was lit, Robin shouted, "Make a wish, Grandma. Make a wish. Wish for something really good. Really, really good. And don't tell anyone or it won't come true. On my hoppy bird-day I wished for something and it came true. Hey, Mom, can you tell your wish after it comes true?"

"Yep," Amy said. "What did you wish for?"

"Okay, but should I whisper my wish or say loud?"

"Loud," Dee said. "Say loud."

"I wished I could fly. I was thinking flying like a bird. But I did fly in an airplane. So see, Grandma, wishes can come true, but maybe not just like you wished them. It can be a surprise when it comes true."

Dee laughed. "Hey, that's my wish. I wish I could fly. Way up high. Like an eagle."

Robin looked alarmed. Her eyebrows up and her forehead wrinkled. She said, "But, Grandma, if you tell your wish it won't come true. You have to candle-wish another wish."

Dee thought about a wish: a roof that didn't leak, light at the end of the tunnel (no, not that, that could mean you're dead), so maybe just some light in her life, or maybe a friend she could talk to? What should she wish for?

"Grandma, hurry the candle's melting!"

She blew without settling on anything specific. Wishes and horoscopes, what did they mean anyway? Although, with wishes you had a moment to consider what was important to you—what mattered. World peace? Yes, world peace—the perfect reply in a Miss America pageant.

Flying? Did she blow any possibility of flying by saying it out loud?

She pulled the spent candle from her cupcake and licked the pink frosting, intentionally getting a blob on her nose, and pretended not to notice.

"Cherry. And delicious."

They all laughed and then each one of them, including Bessie, followed her lead and got icing on their noses. Amy took a picture.

Her present was a blouse with three-quarter length sleeves, perfect for hiding flabby old arms.

"See, Grandma," Robin said, "I picked the pink one specially for you. Cause you and me, we like pink."

"Good job," Dee said and hugged Robin. "I love it."

"Now, open the big present," Robin said.

As Dee unwrapped the long box, Robin shouted, "See, see, we got you a new window shade!"

In the living room Amy took down the old shade. It disintegrated in her hands, crumbling in a cloud of dust and shards of aged and sunburnt, brownish orange linen. The new shade was thick white plastic. When she put it up, it fell down. Its metal posts weren't quite long enough to stick into both sides of the window frame at once. They tried tugging the round gudgeon at one end of the spool; they pulled at the flat pin on the other end with pliers. It was still too short.

"I'm so sorry, Mom," Amy said. She looked like she was going to cry. "We leave tomorrow morning, so there's no time to exchange it."

"Hey," Dee said, "Amy, it's fine." She looked around the room and smiled. "And do you know what I wished for on the birthday candle? I wished for things to be brighter. And, without that old rotten shade, just look at this room, just look how bright and sunny it is in here."

The shade for the big picture window must have cost a fortune. Cut to size. Nonreturnable. The naked picture window was blasting bright light on the situation. In the dazzling daylight all the old, grungy furniture looked worse, dirtier and shabbier than she could have imagined, but she smiled and hugged her daughter.

21. WINDOW SHADE

"If you cannot get the bird, get one of its feathers."
Danish Proverb

Amy and Robin had flown back home to Wisconsin, and Dee was alone with Bessie again. It was unbearably lonely, but in some ways it was good to get back to their routine, nice to have a quiet life again.

The quiet gave her time to reflect. Parenting. When she thought about some of the things Bessie had done as a parent, she was appalled. There had been so many bumps and bruises that Bessie didn't kiss and make better, because she had been the emotional bruiser. Maybe locking her in the dog run had been expedient? Maybe disdaining Dee's looks was just an honest appraisal?

Dee wondered what kind of parent she herself had been? Perfect, no doubt. But did her daughter and son see it that way? Bessie had made big mistakes, and Dee was careful not to make the same ones. Her kids had never spent time in a dog run. She never criticized the way they looked, but then why would she, they were perfectly nice looking people. So much of what Bessie had done, Dee had done the opposite. Bessie was a super homemaker. Dee was a liberated mom with a job she loved, and a mediocre housekeeper at best. Does each generation learn from the past what not to do to their children, only to make fresh mistakes that they don't even see.

Seeing. Casting a fresh light on life. Moving from a dark past to a bright future. She thought about the living room. It was too bright during the daytime, and without a shade on the picture window it felt creepy at night. Seeing their reflections walking past the black void of the naked window was unnerving, so mostly they stayed in the kitchen and listened to the radio. In the daytime, when Bessie took her nap on the living room couch, Dee convinced her to put a black t-shirt over her eyes so she could sleep.

There had to be something she could do about it that wouldn't cost a fortune. She thought about her father. He had an elegant study, but when he had a problem to solve, he went down into the basement.

Her father's workbench was beneath one of the high small windows near the rafters. Spiders flourished there. A scattering of dead bugs: a centipede, two flies and a single ant, were trapped in the spiders' webs along with tiny balls of spider eggs. Were bugs colonizing inside her stored furniture down here? How did so many bugs get into the basement? Did they come in the window? She couldn't see any gaps or spaces where they could get inside. Sy would have freaked out and run upstairs swatting at his hair, vaguely feeling something crawling on him.

Their basement had a small room, a coal bin with a window that once had a coal chute, where years ago a truck would come and dump a load of coal down the chute into the room. The homeowner would then shovel the coal into the potbellied furnace with its opened door, a mouth waiting to be fed on cold winter days. The coal bin was still there in the basement of the Ellison's house, but there was neither coal nor coal burning furnace, just a little room coated with black soot. Could it still be called the coal bin, if it hadn't had coal since just after her parents bought the house and put in a gas furnace? She wondered why they had never cleaned it out. Maybe it was because they never needed the extra space, or maybe because they had better things to do.

Her father's workbench was just a few feet from the door to the coal bin. She sat on Jack Ellison's stool and picked up his metal tackle box. Inside were feathers, embroidery floss, thread, fishing hooks, bits of fur and wool. A magnifying glass on a stand sat on the bench. She remembered sitting for hours watching her father tie flies. He golfed because it was good for business, he fished because he liked the quiet, but mostly he loved tying flies.

She'd asked him if the fish thought it was a little bird landing on the water, and if so wouldn't the fish hide so the bird wouldn't eat it. No, he said, you use the bird feathers to trick the fish into thinking it's a bug and they come to the surface to eat it.

Her father liked making things, working with his hands. He built her a dollhouse from scraps of wood, a small replica of the cottage they'd had for many years on Lower Straits Lake. The real cottage was made of half logs and just had two rooms. The front room seemed like it might have been an enclosed porch with windows on three sides. There was a Formica kitchen table and four chairs at one end of the room, and at the other end of the room there was a sink, an old stove, and a refrigerator. The back room had two double bed mattresses and a toilet in a closet in the corner. It was a humble place that they all loved.

Rather than a dollhouse that opened at the back so you could see all the floors, Jack built Dee's little cottage with a roof that lifted off and you could look down inside. She'd spent hours down the basement "helping" her father. They painted the cottage's sides, shading thick brown stripes on their undersides so they looked like three-dimensional logs. They painted the roof green just like the real cottage.

One evening when Jack went down to the basement to work with his lures, she heard him yell and then he came thundering up the stairs, "Where is he!" He shouted. "Where's Georgie?" She helped her parents search for her brother, who was probably about six at that time. She searched the garage, under his bed, and far back in his closet. They finally found him hiding in the coal bin, so black with soot that he was hard to make out in the dark room. And there on her father's workbench the delicate flies and feathers were all torn to bits. Bessie put Georgie in the bathtub with bubbles where he played and soaked for an hour. Jack left the house. She overheard later that he'd walked his anger off all the way to town where he sat in a bar and had two beers and then walked home. He informed Georgie that he was no longer allowed in the basement. A padlock was added to the door the next day, it wasn't removed until Georgie was in high school.

Dee searched through a box of wood scraps until she found two shims. She used the vice and a handsaw to cut an inch off the thin end of each, then took the cut pieces upstairs and nailed them into the sides of the living room window and reattached the brackets. When she hung the new window shade, it worked. She pulled it down, released it, and it rolled back up. She pulled it down again. Amy's window shade worked and that would make her daughter happy. It was, after all, an excellent gift.

Because there was a slight gap at each side of the window, two lines of light fell across the room. If she were a cat, she'd slap at them with her paw. She studied the lines running across the oriental carpet, up the side of a chair, over cushions, and up the far wall.

An image of sun stripes came into her mind and she stood motionless staring at the floor, holding onto, grasping tight onto a memory.

The bedroom window in her house in Indian Village had venetian blinds, and in the late afternoon the open slats sent stripes of sunlight across their bed. She remembered how they'd dash up the stairs on Saturday or Sunday afternoons and strip naked. They hurried to catch the fleeting minutes before the lines disappeared as the sun moved. They watched the stripes of bright yellow-white light and blue-gray shadow bend over the contours of their bodies: over a hip, down a waist, around a shoulder. They traced their fingers over the light lines on each other. And then they made love.

Sy (sigh). She missed him.

22. THE COTTAGE

"The bird ought not to soil its own nest."
French Proverb

"Will you take me home now," Bessie had her coat on and her purse in hand.

"Traverse City?" Dee asked.

"Yes. You can meet my mother."

Bessie must be feeling homesick. Time for a little distraction again? Dee was going a little stir crazy herself, so a drive might make her feel better too. Not that she planned on driving two hundred and fifty miles up to Traverse City, but why not go see the property they used to own.

Since spending time in the basement at her father's workbench, she'd been thinking about the cottage. The land they'd owned sloped down from a dirt road, down a hill of mown lawn, on down to flat dry land that merged into wetland, past cattails and swamp. A dock, maybe a hundred feet long, stretched over the soggy ground out to a small inlet of Lower Straits Lake.

*

A couple of years after her father died, she had driven Bessie out to see the cottage. It was the first time that Dee was aware of Bessie's memory becoming fuzzy. It had startled her, made her feel a little off balance.

The day stuck in Dee's memory.

"Dee, let's go up to the cottage?" Bessie had said back then. "We could take a picnic lunch, and if there's ducks on the lake we could feed them. And just so's you know, I think the place could use a good cleaning. It's been a while since we were up there."

The cottage—the two-room cabin that her father had copied in dollhouse form for her so many years ago—was long gone.

"It'd be a nice drive, don't you think, Dee? It's a pretty day. Let's have an outing."

"But, Bessie, we don't own it anymore. Remember. It was sold when I was in college."

"Oh." Bessie said, and looked flummoxed. "Oh, right. It's not ours anymore. But couldn't we just drive up there anyway and look around. Maybe we'd see a farm stand and we could buy some corn or tomatoes."

It wasn't that far away, thirty or forty minutes, maybe. So Dee agreed.

"We had nice times up there," Bessie said.

"We did. I remember all of us lying on a blanket on the hill at night and looking at the stars. Dippers...big and little."

"North star," Bessie said.

"And the red planet. And falling stars shooting through the sky," Dee added. "Remember how we made wishes on falling stars."

Bessie was chatty as they drove past subdivisions and strip malls and mega office buildings.

"And there was an old, really old truck, a model T or something like that, all nasty and rusty that you kids liked to climb on. Do you remember that, Dee?"

"Yep. A swarm of bees came out of the tail pipe and chased us."

"I remember how you picked up Georgie and ran into the cottage with him. And, Dee, I don't think you were all that much bigger than him at that time."

"We did have fun though, didn't we? Georgie was always nicer and less of a brat there."

"Georgie was a sweet boy, Dee. You just don't remember. Probably because you got brain damaged in the car accident."

Brat? Or a sweet boy? We are each so subjective, Dee thought. But, actually, pleasant memories of her younger brother lived in that old cottage. Most of the time all she remembered about growing up with Georgie was his meanness, his pranks, his destructiveness. But at the lake she remembered him helping her catch tadpoles, and chasing frogs along the edge of the grasses. This was where Georgie became a little brother like her friends' little brothers, happy and silly and someone different than Georgie at home.

"I think he liked the fishing. Your dad and Georgie would go out in the evening and dig for worms, night crawlers, and put them in an old coffee can. You remember how there were two double beds in the sleeping room? Georgie and your father would sleep in the one closest to the door, so they wouldn't wake us up when they got up early to fish. They'd go out at five in the morning and be out there until nine or ten, hours and hours just sitting in a rowboat. I can't imagine doing that."

"I don't remember them ever catching anything."

"A snapping turtle, once. Maybe some fish that they threw back because they were too little. Just so's you know, Dee, I was always glad that they didn't bring back any fish for me to clean."

When they arrived at the property, Dee had pulled over to the side of the road and they sat and stared out the window.

"Is this the right place? This can't be the right place," Bessie said.

A wide concrete driveway ran down the hill to a garage in front of a modern house, all very new, white and pristine, even the driveway looked like a recent pour. The whole neighborhood was different. The dirt road was paved. No longer country, it was a community of full time residences. The cottage was gone.

"There used to be empty fields around here where we picked wild strawberries, remember that, Bessie?"

"Things change," Bessie said. "Things get old and get replaced with new things. People too."

"Tell me about it," Dee said. "Let's get out and walk around a bit. Stretch our legs after sitting so long."

They got out of the car, but then just stood beside it. There were no sidewalks, so they just stood there for a minute and then got back in the car. Dee started the engine and they headed home.

"Your father blamed Georgie," Bessie had said.

"Huh?"

"It was after Georgie had his driver's license, and he had a car. Remember that red car your dad got him?"

"What did Dad blame him for?"

"Well, just so's you know, Dee, I never agreed with Jack about Georgie being to blame."

"Blame for what?"

"We decided to sell the cottage that fall. I remember it was fall because we raked leaves. We weren't coming up here all that much anymore—you kids were busy with your own lives with your friends and all that. You were in college then, weren't you?"

"Yeah," Dee said. "Remember how we used to talk on Saturday mornings? I think either you or dad told me the cottage was sold on a phone call. Actually, I'm pretty sure it was you who told me. It made me sad. The cottage was always a happy place, but then we really hadn't been there in a while. Not me, anyway."

"So, well, we cleaned up the cottage real nice, in fact Georgie was cleaning with us, and he was working hard too. We painted the inside, raked the leaves, pulled weeds, and I got a fresh piece of blue and white checked oilcloth for the kitchen table. It looked real cute." She stopped then and looked at Dee. "I don't remember you helping with it? Where were you, anyway?"

Dee shook her head. She had just said she was away at school. Bessie either wasn't listening or was really losing it.

"I must have been at Michigan State."

"Hmm, yes. Just so's you know, I still don't believe it was Georgie."

"What? What? Tell me what happened?"

"Okay. Okay. You're so impatient, Dee."

"Sorry. Go on."

"Well, we had a couple interested in buying it, so we drove them out there to show it to them, but when we got there it was a wreck. Somebody had vandalized it. The police said it was probably teenagers, since there were beer cans and nasty used, you know, those...those things for birth control that men wear. All the windows, every single one of them was broken, completely gone, with the smashed glass all over the floor. Birds were flying in and out like the cottage was just part of the countryside. Someone had bashed in the wall of that little room the toilet was in. It was just a mess."

"How awful. And the potential buyers were there seeing it all. What a mess. Dad must have been mortified."

"And even worse, someone had gone tuzzy wuzzy on one of the mattresses. Disgusting. Shameful."

"Pooped?"

"Don't say that. Say tuzzy wuzzy or geeze."

"Geeze sounds worse than poop. Poop just sounds like a plop, it's quick and it's done, but geeze is disgusting—greasy, slow, messy. And tuzzy wuzzy sounds like a kid's stuffed animal. The little boy slept with his tuzzy wuzzy every night."

"Ick. That's nasty. I still don't like that other word."

"Which word?"

"Ha! Dee, you're trying to trick me into saying poop, and I won't say it. So there!"

Dee laughed.

"What?"

But Dee didn't tell her.

"Doctors say 'stool' or bowel movement," Dee offered.

"I don't like that either," Bessie said. "Stool sounds like something covered in chintz or tapestry that you put your feet on, and the other one sounds like a dance or a concert inside your body."

"Huh?"

"The movement one," Bessie said. "Dee, just so's you know, I really rather we say tuzzy wuzzy?"

"Okay. So which mattress got tuzzy wuzzied?"

"The boys' mattress. The one your dad and Georgie slept on."

"And Dad blamed Georgie?"

"Yes," Bessie said. "When we got home, he screamed and yelled at him. Georgie was out really late one night with his friends, and Jack said he smelled beer on him, that's why Jack thought he did it. He took away his car. Sold it."

"Oh geez."

"I didn't think Georgie would'a done it because he worked so hard helping us clean it up to sell. Jack said Georgie was mad at us for wanting to sell it. But I really don't think he did it."

"So then the people didn't buy it?"

"Your father was so mad and upset that he said he didn't even want to look at the place anymore, ever again. He sold it 'as is'. Later we figured out that they just wanted the land anyway, but because it was so disgusting of a mess, they got the price way down."

"Well, if Georgie did it, it didn't work out for him, since you sold it anyway."

"Georgie wouldn't a done it, Dee. I know it wasn't him. Maybe the people who bought it came out there and made a mess just so's they could get it cheaper. That's what I always thought."

"How come I never heard about this before?"

"You're father was so upset, he said no one was to ever mention the cottage again. Ever. He even said we were only to tell you that it was sold, and that was that. He didn't want you to know about the mess."

*

As Dee drove Bessie north, toward the old site of the long gone cottage, she thought about how much Bessie had declined since that trip so many years ago. Would she remember any of it? Would she be able to carry on such an involved conversation now, particularly if it didn't involve what was for lunch? And she wondered if Georgie had really done it—tuzzy-wuzzy and destruction. It was easy to blame him. George Ellison, all public charm and charisma—was still an angry, spoiled little boy.

She was driving toward the cottage, or where the cottage used to be, but when she stopped at a red light, Bessie (who had forgotten about driving to Traverse City) asked, "So, anyways, Dee, where are we going?"

Dee asked herself what the point was. There was nothing to see there, no vestige of her youth. So she turned the car around, and said, "Home."

23. ZITA

*"A bird that you set free may be caught again,
but a word that escapes your lips will not return."*
Jewish Proverb

On June 10th, Dee and Bessie sat on the front porch thinking, Bessie was anyway, about what they'd have for lunch.

"Bologna with cottage cheese in the middle, rolled up like a hot dog. That would be good, don't you think, Dee?" Bessie said.

"Oh, delicious," Dee said, and rolled her eyes. "Except we don't have any bologna or cottage cheese." She was feeling snappy, and cranky, alone with Bessie, as always. She missed Robin and Amy.

She was trying to convince Bessie that peanut butter and jelly sandwiches would be the most delicious of all lunch choices (or how about a big bowl of oatmeal with banana, which was much healthier than bologna), when a red Miata convertible pulled into the driveway. Zita, Georgie's wife, sat in the driver's seat with her hair all wild and wind blown. Maybe that isn't Zita, Dee thought. Her sister-in-law never had messy hair, and this woman was peering into her rear view mirror and intentionally roughing up her black hair. As she climbed out of the little car, Dee first saw sparkly flip flops that caught the sunlight and sent out beams of light below the open car door, and then ankles in very tight jeans. As she stood, the full body came into sight in a snug tee shirt. Yes, it was Zita, of course. Dee looked down at her own thick hams, and prepared herself for a round of feeling less because she was more—more bulk, more flab, more insecure.

Bessie said, "Hello, Dear." Her tone was so happy, so loving, that Dee wanted to get up and leave the porch. Just walk. Head down the street, don't look back, climb a fence and fly away.

As Zita came up the porch stairs, her bejeweled flip flops made a plopping sound with each step she took. Zita always had noisy feet, high heels clacking, and today she wore noisy sandals with beads glued on the straps.

The grand Ms. Z said, "Well, I'm glad to see you're both here."

Dee thought, anywhere we are, we're both there. Always. Always. Always. But she smiled, or anyway her lips turned up at the outside edges. She took a sip of her coffee but didn't offer a cup to her sister-in-law, still remembering the last time Zita came to the house and the coffee disaster.

She said, "Zita, if you're here to tell me I have to pay for a new suit for Georgie, you're barking up the wrong tree."

"What?" Zita scowled, and Dee wanted to mention that scowling could give you wrinkles. She was already in a bad mood, and this was the last thing she needed.

"I'm not paying for a new suit for Georgie. The coffee spill was as much his fault as mine." *So there*, she thought, but didn't say it.

"I don't know what you're talking about." Zita said.

"Georgie sent me a note that said, 'you owe me $3,500 for my ruined suit'."

Zita shook her head. "I'm sorry," she said. "I didn't know anything about that. But he did tell me that you called him asking him to help pay for a new roof. He said that your roof was leaking."

"Yes, and he basically told me to go to hell."

"Dee!" Bessie shouted, "Ugly. Ugly talk."

Dee looked directly at Bessie and said, not loud, not shouted, but in a calm and quiet, although challenging tone, "hell."

"I'm here about the roof," Zita said. "You know that my brother Joey is a contractor, so I'm going to have him come out and look at your roof."

Joey Spinelli. Dee felt her face flush. Zita and Georgie's wedding. A one-night stand in her youth—a wedding night stand. Standing. He never called, so she forgot it. She hadn't seen him in decades. And now Zita was going to have him come to the house and see her wrinkles. But then, he was probably wrinkled too—with a big gut, bald, and a big brown wart on his nose.

"I can't afford it," Dee said, "And why would you do that anyway. What do you care? Are you strumming up business for your brother?"

Bessie said, "Dee, you're being rude." Her voice timid, she wasn't used to Dee being in such openly bad humor.

Zita pinched her lips together, shook her head. "Look, Dee, I'm actually wanting to help. Your brother is a mother fucking son of a bitch." She stopped suddenly and looked at Bessie, "I'm sorry, Bessie. Excuse my language."

"I'm going to go in and watch the TV now." Bessie said, and stood. "Too much ugly talk out here."

They watched as Bessie, slumped and forlorn, carried her cane into the house and slammed the screen door. But behind the door she said loudly, "It's disgraceful to say bad things about your own husband to others. Disgraceful, just so's you know, I don't like it, not any one little bit.

"Sit," Dee said to Zita and pointed at Bessie's chair. "She won't remember how to turn the TV on. I'll be right back."

Dee got her mother settled on the couch watching a game show.

"I don't understand how that woman can be so mean about Georgie, and I don't want to hear any more ugly talk."

"I'll make the TV louder."

Dee was anxious to get back out on the porch and hear more ugly talk. Zita ranting about Georgie, made Dee like her a little and softened her bad mood, so before going back outside she went to the kitchen and poured a cup of coffee. Zita would take it black, she guessed—zero calories.

On the porch she handed her sister-in-law the cup and sat down beside her.

"Okay, so what's going on?" she asked.

"He's a son of a bitch."

"So what's new?"

"And this isn't the first time. It's been over and over and over. But I'm telling you this. This is the last time," Zita said, and punched her right fist into her left palm.

Last time what? Dee wanted to ask, but just kept her mouth shut and let the woman rant. She didn't coo, or nod or sympathize. Just listened and waited.

"This time it's different. This time she's suing the bastard. This time I'm divorcing the bastard. That's it!" And again she smacked her fist into her palm with a pop. Too hard this time, she shook out her punched palm.

"He fired her, and now she's suing him for..." here Zita made air quotes, "for expecting her to do inappropriate things that were against her ethics."

"Ginger?" Dee said out loud, and then wanted to slap her hand over her mouth. She shouldn't know about Ginger, and why, oh why did she still remember her name? Why? She was wholesome, or at least looked wholesome, which wasn't necessarily a judgment on her behavior. Her hair color could have come out of a bottle on the spice rack. Ginger? No, real ginger, the spice, was more yellow. Ginger, the woman, had hair more like the color of cinnamon. And her freckles could have been dotted on with a burnt sienna fine-tipped marker.

Zita stopped her rant, and stared at Dee.

"You knew?"

"Guessed."

"You didn't tell me?" She looked hurt, but then smiled at Dee. "Oh, never mind. Why would you tell me? He's your brother and we—you and I—haven't exactly been friends."

"I'm sorry," Dee said, and then wondered what she was being sorry for. That they weren't friends?

"I'd like to kill him," Zita said.

How can I help, Dee thought, but didn't say.

"I could cut the brake line in his car," Zita said, "and film him going over a cliff."

"I know right where the brake lines are," Dee said. "I could show you." Her penciling career left her with excellent knowledge of car guts.

"But there aren't any cliffs around here, and besides, I don't want to go to prison. And you don't either, Missy." Zita laughed then, and said, "Hey, remember that day we were here, the day you threw coffee at him?"

"It was an accident," Dee said.

"Yeah, yeah, whatever." Zita said, and flapped both hands in the air. Zita spoke Italian, but only with her hands, although her family was Italian, third generation.

"Maybe your brother, Joey, the contractor, could make Georgie some concrete socks?" Dee said.

Zita stared at Dee, and Dee was sure she'd made a mistake. She'd just slandered all Italians. She wished she could take the words back. But Zita started laughing.

"Good one," Zita said, "but Joey'd never do it. I like the idea myself. Get him into concrete socks, push him into his fucking penis pool and watch him sink—blub, blub. Little bubbles floating to the surface and then none."

Startled, Dee laughed, and asked, "Did he intentionally have the pool look like that?"

"You know your brother. What do you think?"

Zita sipped her coffee, sighed, and said, "I don't really want to kill him. I used to love him, you know." Then she swigged the coffee back like a shot of Scotch, shook her head, and wiped her mouth with the back of her hand. "Not any more."

"So, Okay, Dee, here's the thing. When we were here that day, and you told me how you had paid off your father's second mortgage, I realized then what a scumbag your brother is. Well, I already knew it, but that was the straw. Well, it was the straw before the Ginger straw, which was really the last straw."

Dee looked at Zita with a question-marked expression.

"Your father must have taken out that second mortgage for Georgie. He loaned him the money to save us from going bankrupt. When Jack lost his memory, Georgie told me that the good part of that was that he'd never have to pay back the loan. Maybe he just assumed your dad was rolling in money? Basically you ended up paying for Georgie's loan. Then he was afraid that you'd find the IOU he had signed with your father."

"So that's why he had his secretary searching through my dad's files that day. He had Ginger do unethical things. Hmph."

"Oh, I'm sure there were more unethicals," Zita said. "Years of lending money to people who he knew, HE KNEW, wouldn't be able to pay—no doc, no document loans—and then those people—who he'd convinced that they could afford the loans—lost everything. People trust bankers, you know. Mortgage lenders are in the same category. Anyway, they trust that when a mortgage company gives them money, that the company expects them to be able to pay back the loan, so why would they give them more of a loan than they can expect to get paid back? They're tricked into buying more house than they can afford. And then they lose it. Kinda like trusting your priest with your children. Ha! Right? But seriously, people just expect the best from them. Those mortgage people know things you don't and you just trust that they're doing the right thing."

Dee didn't say anything. Just listened.

"He didn't care," Zita went on. "It didn't hurt him, those loans were bundled off and he never thought about them again. Nobody knows anymore who owns their mortgage. I know this crap first-hand, I worked at the office a few years ago. But then he didn't like my comments about what he was doing to people. And also I cramped his style with the female employees. He's a greedy bad man, Dee. I know you probably don't like hearing that about your brother, but it's true."

"How much did my father loan him?"

"Over a hundred thousand."

Dee already knew how much it was, but still, hearing the number made her angry. She knew the second mortgage had taken her over a decade to pay off. A decade of skipping drinks and lunches out with her co-workers—always a brown bag at her desk; a decade of miserly water and electric usage; a decade of few new clothes; a decade of diligently paying off her father's debt; a decade of scrounging.

"Georgie cheats people, he cheated me," Zita said. "Cheated on me." She touched Dee's hand then. "He cheated you."

"Your Dad came to our house, several times," she continued, "before his ulcer exploded, and basically begged Georgie to start paying back the loan. Georgie would promise and then ignore him. Hide out. Not answer the door when Jack would show up. Jack would say that he hated that his son was so irresponsible about his debt. And that made me think that Jack didn't need the money, but that he just wanted his son to act right. When we all thought your dad would die in surgery, Georgie seemed relieved. I think that's when I started hating him."

Dee just shook her head, she felt stunned. She had spent years blaming her father for being reckless with money, Jack Ellison—Mr. Big Spender. Instead he was Jack Ellison—Georgie's father, helping out his son.

"Anyway, Dee. I haven't filed for divorce yet. My lawyer says, 'Be smart.' I haven't let on to Georgie that I plan to leave him." She clasped her hands together and shook them in front of her chest. "So I'm planning to wipe him out. First off, you're getting a new roof. Georgie will pay for it, although he won't know it."

Zita opened her purse and took out a little notebook, she wrote on it, tore out the page and handed it to Dee. "My cell number, Georgie never answers it, so if you need anything call me."

"Okay. But Zita, did Bessie know about the loan?"

"No, your father was clear on that. He said he didn't want her fretting about anything. He adored your mother. Sheltered her."

"So, wait," Dee said, "What was the signature about? Georgie was trying to get Bessie's signature. Why?"

"I guess so that if you ever found the IOU, he'd have a forged note from Bessie saying that he'd paid off the loan."

"Or the other possibility was to have Ginger find the IOU and he could get rid of it." Dee said.

Zita leaned toward Dee and said in a hushed tone, "By the way, Dee, if my father was still alive, Georgie would be hanging out with Jimmy Hoffa somewhere under the foundation of a high rise."

*

When Zita left, Dee remained sitting on the front porch. She could hear the loud TV in the living room, and knew that Bessie would be expecting her to come sit with her. That is, if Bessie even remembered that Zita had stopped by, Dee would have to hear all about her mother's distaste for precious Georgie's nasty wife.

But Dee needed to process what had just happened. Zita was going to leave Georgie, wipe him out, help Dee pay for a roof, or rather Georgie would be paying for his mother's new roof. Zita said she had a plan.

So would Zita actually leave Georgie? Georgie was an ass, an adulterer, corrupt, but they'd been married for forty years. If she let Zita's brother fix the roof would she end up with a huge bill? She never trusted Georgie, and her only experience with Zita was as part of his team.

Could she trust her? Should she trust her? She was never someone Dee liked. Never-ever. What if this was some scheme that Georgie had cooked up? What if he had sent his wife in on a reconnaissance mission? Gather information. But actually, Zita came with information. Was it all a trick or a treat?

24. POWER OF ATTORNEY

"Do not count your chickens before they are hatched."
Aesop

It's nice to have a lawyer who makes house calls.

After Zita told Dee about the money Georgie had borrowed from their father, Dee contacted her lawyer, Ray. A few days later he came to the house with his assistant, Cara. He said they should take care of some other paperwork too. When they were all comfortably gathered around the dining room table, Ray asked. "Bessie, are you good with assigning your power of attorney to Dee?"

"Does that mean she's my attorney? I thought you were the attorney?"

"No," Ray said, "It just means that if you become incapacitated, she can pay your bills."

"Well," Bessie said, "Just so's you know, she's been doing that for a long time already, without me signing any paper."

"This would make it legal for her to make decisions if you couldn't."

Bessie shrugged, tilted her head to one side and smiled. "Okay, we can do that."

"And what about an Advance Directive? How do you want to be cared for at the end? This is also referred to as a Living Will. Would you want Dee to decide what medical treatment you should get, if you can't. Say if you're too ill or unconscious?"

"Do you mean I'm signing these papers so that she can pull the plug?"

There was uncomfortable laughter around the table.

"Yes," Ray said. "You would be telling the hospital that she can decide whether to pull the plug or not."

"I've had a good life, just so's you know. And Dee is mostly good to me. She gets a little cranky now and then, but I trust her. She knows I want the plug pulled."

"Okay then." Ray said and started putting x's on forms where Bessie and Dee should sign.

When the flutter of papers subsided, Ray said, "Okay then, now about your will. You and your husband have a will that divides everything equally between your two children. However, it seems that your husband lent your son George a hundred thousand dollars, and that George never repaid anything on that loan."

"No," Bessie said. "Just so's you know, Jack woulda never have done that. He made good money, but I'm pretty sure we never had that much in our savings."

"Actually he took out a second mortgage on the house. And over the years Dee repaid that loan. So I'm thinking that the fair thing to do would be to change the will, so that the children still divide the estate, but George gets a hundred thousand less."

Bessie contemplated. She fidgeted in her chair. She sipped her iced tea. She lifted sheets of paper and put them back down.

"I'm thinking," Bessie finally said, "that over all these years, Dee got to live in this nice house, so what she paid out was like rent. This is a really big, lovely house. I'm sort of hurt that Jack never told me about this loan, though. Do you have any idea why he didn't tell me?"

Ray shook his head.

"But Georgie probably needed the money to support that fancy wife of his with her beaded shoes. So no. No changes. I want to leave the will just as my husband had it. We just divide everything equally."

With her left hand she reached over to her right side and grabbed the black cane that was propped against her chair. She held it up to show the gold tip and said to everyone at the table, "See this cane? That top piece, that's real gold. This was my father's cane. He had it made after he panned for gold in Colorado when he was a young man. This gold handle came from the actual gold he found. And that bottom bit there, that's iron or something strong. And you know what?"

She stopped then, waiting for someone to ask *what*.

Ray said, "What?"

"This cane reminds me of my father. He was a good strong man, good as gold. I'd like you to put in the will that Georgie gets this cane."

25. SEX

"Keep a green tree in your heart
and perhaps the singing bird will come."
Chinese Proverb

Zita's brother, Joey Spinelli, the roofing contractor—forty years had definitely changed him, grayed him. He was shorter than Dee by at least an inch, built tight and solid, no beer gut. No big brown wart anywhere that she could see. Not bad for a man in his late sixties. He wore a crisp white T-shirt—new, still with the hard creases from the package. In the front hall he bent down and removed his work boots. *Unnecessary*, she said. *Habit*, he said. He smelled clean, maybe like Ivory soap, the soap that floats. His blue eyes watched her so intently that she felt herself contract and thaw. She stared back at those blue eyes and all she could think about was *doing him*, as she'd heard people say on TV. Doing him. Sex. She blushed, felt the heat run rampant all over her face and down her torso. He probably didn't even remember the coatroom. A moment in time, lost in an alcoholic haze. He never called her.

She was sixty-five years old, and she still noticed men. Men on TV shows, men in stores, and men on underwear packages. She insisted that Bessie walk with her up and down every aisle in Costco, including all the clothing aisles, where she pretended not to be looking at the four packs of men's underpants. Pictures of male models with their lumpy briefs made her want to stop and examine the package photo—look closely, but of course, she couldn't do that without her mother or anyone else catching her. Tighty-whitey's were gross, but those fitted underpants that came down a man's legs were very sexy. Dark colors. Boxers on the other hand were just silly, loosey goosey, although she'd heard that they were best to keep a man's sperm cool and fresh, able to make babies.

She thought about Joey Spinelli touching her—it'd been such a long time since any man had touched her. What would it be like to lay in stripes of sunshine with him? She imagined herself running her index finger up a sun line on his hip and over his...

"So," Joey said, "I'm anxious to get up in there."

She blushed, embarrassed—what he was talking about? She hadn't been listening—too occupied with a fantasized future to know what he was saying in the now.

"I'm gonna need to look around up there," he said.

Up in there? Look around?

He shook his head slightly and looked at her quizzically. Jesus, he probably thought she was a demented old woman. They were around the same age, he was Zita's oldest brother. There was no explaining attraction. He was short. Sy had been four inches taller than her. But did size really matter?

"Hello," he said. "Are you there, Dee." Then he laughed.

So she laughed too. "Sorry," she said. When in doubt be honest, right? "What were you saying?" but not completely honest.

He probably had this happen with women all the time. It was a wonder he got anything done. Women probably swooned over him like he was some rock star, unable to speak or answer his questions.

"Attic." he said, "I should check your attic."

"Oh, attic," she said, and raised her hand and pointed. "It's upstairs." Upstairs! Of course it was upstairs. Where else would an attic be? Downstairs? It was possible that she would faint from embarrassment any minute. Then die. This is how it happens. That's why there's the phrase, *died of embarrassment*. Bessie would outlive her after all.

Instead of dying, she laughed. "In case you're wondering, the basement's downstairs." and she pointed down.

He moved his big phallic flashlight to his left hand, took hold of her pointing finger, moved it so it pointed up, and said softly, "Dee, lead the way."

Was he going to hold her finger all the way upstairs? Nope, he let go and she walked in front of him, worried about how her butt looked. Was it too wide? Was it flabby? Her body was way past its "use by" date.

The stairs always left her breathless when she got to the top of the flight, so she tried to control her breathing. What if she hyperventilated and had to breathe into a bag?

On the second floor, he said, "First off, why don't you show me which rooms have leaks?"

She led him into her bedroom, looked at her neatly made bed and felt a little vaginal tug. *Do him.* She felt the heat rise up her neck and cover her face, and quickly turned away from him. She could always claim it was a hot flash, even though she hadn't had one in years. Good to be over hot flashes, but awful to be too old for them.

Cool it, she told herself. *You're going to freak the man out.*

"Oh yeah," he said, staring into the bucket, then looking at the gray spot on the ceiling. "Hey, Dee, I think you should know..." he hesitated.

"Yes?"

"Your roof's been leaking."

Joey Spinelli—kidder. A funny guy.

"Ha ha. Thanks for telling me."

"Hey..." he said, but then hesitated, like what he wanted to say made him nervous. Finally, he asked, "Do you remember Zita and Georgie's wedding?"

Did she remember?

It was over forty years ago, she was twenty-four and still single when her younger brother got married. Maybe because Georgie and Zita were so young—just eighteen and twenty respectively—there was a rumor that Zita was pregnant and it was a shotgun wedding, but it turned out to be just a rumor.

The bridesmaids' dresses created a rainbow: pink, lavender, pale blue, green, lemon, tangerine and rose. Of course, Dee was the bridesmaid Zita chose for the fru-fru pond scum green gown with a hoop skirt. Dee hated it. Little Bo Peep in dead frog green.

Joey—one of the groomsmen—sat next to her at the reception. There was a lot of toasting with champagne and flirting, and then wine and flirting with dinner, and then shots and beers and more flirting, and dancing and more flirting.

She had a foggy alcohol-slurred memory of an unattended coatroom, shifting hangers, handsome Joe Spinelli in a black tux with satin lapels lifting the ugly green chiffon and the hoop, and then disappearing under all the layers of her skirts—a groomsman taking advantage of a drunken bridesmaid? Not many women would think so. Considering...

Joey Spinelli—no wonder her reaction to him was visceral.

"Yes. I remember." Blush.

"I called and left messages with your mother a bunch of times after that," he said. "I liked you." He didn't add *you were delicious.*

"I never got any messages," she said. Of course, her mother wouldn't give her Joey's messages—he was Italian *and* Catholic. It was bad enough that her precious son married Zita.

"I'm so sorry. I liked you too," she said.

"So, now here we are forty years later, a couple of old farts," he said. "And you have a leaking roof. Any more leaks?"

She didn't mention the occasional leak when she sneezed—the panty liners kept her secret.

"There's WikiLeaks?" she said.

"Good one," he said and touched her shoulder.

"Yeah, I think someone's been hacking into the roof, there's also another leak in Georgie's old room. Do you think it could have been Julian Assange?" Now she was showing off. She told herself to shut up.

"You read the paper. Good," he said.

She led him down the hall to Georgie's room, where they both looked up at the ceiling, then down at the bucket.

"Dee, would you consider getting a cup of coffee sometime with an old fart."

"Any old fart in particular?" She asked, and grinned at him.

"No, no one in particular."

"Jerk."

He laughed. "Okay, so me, in particular."

"What would your wife say?"

She watched his shoulders sag, and sorrow filled his face.

"Hmm." he said, "so, tell me this, how can a family be so disjointed? We are family, you know, you and me. I'm your brother's brother-in-law, and I've been widowed for four years."

"I didn't know that, Joey. I'm very sorry."

"I'm okay. Mary was sick for years."

Just a month after she eloped with Sy, Mary and Joseph had a big Catholic wedding, and a joke went around that they were riding a camel to their honeymoon site in a manger.

His shoulders returned to where they belonged, and he asked again, "Coffee out with me sometime?"

"I'd like that," she said. "But I don't know how."

"You just put on your shoes and walk out the door."

She looked down at her bare feet—bunions, pink toenails.

"No," she said, and shook her head and wanted to weep. "I can't leave my mother home alone. She wanders."

"Maybe someone could come sit with her?"

"There's no one. But I make good coffee. You could come here." And then she wondered how Bessie would treat him. He was Italian and Catholic.

*

When Joey Spinelli climbed up into the attic, Dee didn't follow or lead, or even stick her head up into the opening. After he finished crawling around on joists and descended down through the little door in the ceiling of her mother's bedroom closet, there were cobwebs in his hair. She thought about gently brushing them away, but hesitated. He felt them and swept his hand across his face and then through his gray hair. She could still say, you missed some and have a reason to touch him, but again, she hesitated.

He explained how the location of the leak in her bedroom ceiling wasn't necessarily directly beneath a hole in the roof, that water found its own course.

"Like it wanted to drip right on my face."

"Exactly."

Outside he pulled a ladder off his truck, then with it leaning against the house he climbed up, pushed away from the building, rattled the extension, muscled it up, and then he climbed up on the roof and walked around— he was in harmony with heights. Dee stood on the lawn with Bessie. She held her breath.

"What's that man doing up there, Dee?" Bessie asked. "Do we know him? Did I give him permission to do that, to walk around on my ceiling?"

"That's Joey, Bessie. You know, Zita's brother. He's going to fix our roof. Remember?"

"What's wrong with our roof?"

"Leaking. Remember?" Dee said, "Buckets in my bedroom and Georgie's old room. Remember."

Bessie got that look, the defensive/defiant one. "Yes, of course, I remember. Dee, I'm not going senile, you know."

"I know, Bessie. You've got all your marbles."

"Georgie had white marbles in a bowl, remember that, Dee? I wonder why he never comes to visit me? Do you think I did something to hurt his feelings? I wonder what I did?"

Then she looked back up at the man on the roof and pointed.

"Well, did your father talk to that man? You can't always trust handymen, you know. Jack should be out here to watch him up there. He'd make sure that man's doing a good job."

Dee didn't say anything or react in any way. *Let it go, just let it go. In five minutes or an hour, Bessie will be back in the present. Let her have Jack back for a little while.*

When Joey came back down the ladder he only used one hand, in the other was a robin's nest. He held it out to Dee, and said, "A present for you, madam. This little home was abandoned next to the chimney."

Dee said, "I'll treasure it forever."

He told them that there were three layers of roofing up there and the whole thing would have to be stripped down before new shingles could go up. The problem was that there were two other jobs that his crew had to finish before they could start. He'd have his guys come out and put tarps on the roof to keep the weather out until they could do the job.

"Maybe you should tell Jack all this," Bessie said.

Joey looked at Dee. "Jack?"

She was standing slightly behind Bessie, and she gave a slight headshake signal, and said, "My father."

"Ohhh," he said. "Jack. Of course."

And she liked him even more.

"Do you have time for a cup of coffee?" Dee asked.

*

The three of them sat in the kitchen. Bessie had returned to the present and was a widow again. Joey was upgraded from handyman to welcomed guest. Bessie got caught up in Joey's charisma and she became charming, telling stories about her childhood.

After Joey was gone, Bessie said, "He seems like a nice fellow. Do you think he'd like to visit us again?"

"Maybe."

"Dee, I think that he likes you. I saw him looking at you with the sweet eye. It'd be nice for you to have a beau. I'm too old for him myself. But still he's pretty cute, don't you think."

Bessie was all a flutter, chatting, and happily matchmaking. Dee hadn't seen her so jolly in years. Joe Spinelli had an effect on both of them.

"So, how do we know him?" Bessie asked.

"He's Zita's brother. Georgie's wife's brother."

Bessie's features seemed to drop. She frowned and said, "Italian," but then straightened her face, and said,

"Oh, well. We're getting old, Dee, if some nice gentleman comes along, who cares if he's Italian anyway. Beggars can't be choosers."

"We're not beggars," Dee said. But still it seemed like a breakthrough. Bessie, in ninety years of life, had never shown any humanity for any humans that weren't from her limited genetic pool. Was this the grace of old age? Was this a softening? Can compassion be acquired? Whatever it was, Dee was happy and grateful.

26. BREAK-IN

"To scare a bird is not the way to catch it."
French Proverb

Bessie was on the living room couch having her afternoon nap. Dee was sketching fat pigeons crowding out the little birds at the bird feeder outside the window in her father's study when she heard a rattling noise coming from the kitchen. She stopped, her pencil unmoving and her ears alert. She heard the kitchen door creak open. Someone was breaking in. Wasn't that door locked? She was sure that it had been locked—she locked it before bed every night, and she hadn't opened it yet today. Her heart was beating fast. She got up from the chair soundlessly and then stood motionless. Should she hide? What about Bessie? Whoever was breaking into the house might hurt Bessie. And why, why was she more afraid he'd hurt Bessie than she was for herself?

She scanned the study for a weapon. The intruder was in the kitchen with all the knives. Her eye caught on the leather cup on the desk that held pens. A pearl handled letter opener was sticking up. She grabbed it and held it tight in her right hand. If the bad guy had a gun she was shit out of luck.

She should have a cell phone. Why didn't she get a cell phone like everyone else in the world? Her father never wanted a phone in his study, he didn't want to be disturbed, and if there was a call Bessie would answer it in the kitchen and come get him if needed, and so there never was a phone in this room. The only phone on the main floor was the black phone over the counter on the kitchen wall. Of course, the burglar was in the kitchen with the only phone and all the knives. The only other phone in the house was in her parent's bedroom, Bessie's room upstairs. A lot of good those phones did her now. Anyway, he could have cut the phone lines. She really needed a cell phone.

She crept down the hall, grateful that the house was solid and the floorboards didn't creak. She was barefoot as usual and that was a good thing too.

As she neared the kitchen, she wondered if she should raise her arm with the letter opener ready to thrust down, or should she keep her hand down with the weapon concealed? She was too frightened to raise her arm, so she kept her hand at her side with the letter opener tucked in close to her thigh. As she rounded the corner into the dim, shade darkened dining room her elbow bumped the china cabinet and rattled plates.

He stood there in the doorway, a dark shadow figure (rapist, killer, thief) with the bright kitchen behind him, and she screamed. She screamed so loud it hurt her own ears. Even after her eyes adjusted to the light and she recognized him, she screamed again.

"Why didn't you knock or ring the doorbell?" She yelled, fury following fear. "Why couldn't you just ring the damn doorbell?"

Did he think they weren't home? Her car was in the garage, most of the time she just left it out in the driveway, but the birds had been consuming mulberries and pooping purple all over her car. Did he sneak in to search for the IOU?

"Hey, it's my family home too," he said. "Why should I have to knock or ring. Who made you the guard of the doors? I lived here all my childhood."

She pushed past him into the kitchen, laid the letter opener on the counter, filled a glass with water, and drank the whole thing. She turned to face him and asked, "So what do you want, Georgie?" and wiped her mouth with the back of her hand.

"Why was Joe Spinelli's truck in front of this house?"

"None of your business. But I have a question for you. I want to know why you never paid our father back the money you borrowed?"

"What?"

His handsome brow furrowed, his dimples weren't that cute.

"How do you know about that?"

Oh hell, she screwed up. Why did she open her big mouth? She couldn't let him know that Zita told her about the loan. She'd just broken Zita's trust. Would he make a connection with Joey Spinelli and her knowing about the loan?

So she lied. "I found a file that Dad had with your IOU and his notes saying you never paid. That's how I know."

"You're lying. Show me. Show me the damn file."

Yes, of course, she was lying. She had no idea what the IOU looked like, no details to back up her claim. Think quick.

"I gave it to my attorney. But why did you do it? Why did you borrow so much? You obviously never intended to pay him back."

"Why?" he said, and sneered at her. "Why? Daddy's little princess wants to know why? I'll tell you why. Because, I could! I wanted to see if the man who beat me and neglected me, and only did nice things for his precious princess gave a rat's ass about me."

He laughed harshly then. "I didn't even need the money. I just wanted to see if he'd come through."

"And he did," Dee said softly.

"Like hell he did. A week later he started nagging me to pay him back."

"He wrote in his notes that you told him you'd go bankrupt without his money." She was becoming a very good at this. Improv?

Georgie laughed, a bitter evil sound. "Bankrupt? Oh, yeah, that's what I told him. Not true. I'm good with finances. I'm so good with money. Excellent with money."

Is he lying? Zita seemed to believe that they were actually going bankrupt back then. Did he lie to her, too?

Did Georgie buy his penis pool before or after that? It must have been before, since she and Sy had been together then. Why would their father give him all that money when he could see how Georgie used it?

"You should've paid him back," Dee said.

"Bullshit," he bellowed.

"He took out a huge loan to give you that money. This house was all paid off and he took out a loan against the house to help you." Oh, Daddy, what a stupid move, you could have, should have, at the least had him co-sign a bank loan. "How desperate did you act to get him to do that? Did you cry? Waa waa. Did you say, 'you like Dee more than me'?" She listened to her own taunting, childlike, sing-song tone—and liked it.

"Fuck you, Dee! Fuck you!" His voice was loud and menacing and as he said it he leaned in on her. "I'm not giving you a penny."

"You know why he was good to me? Don't you get it, Georgie? It was because I wasn't good enough for Bessie. I wasn't pretty enough for my mother. You were her little prince. So what. It was what it was. You get what you get. But you always had to have more. I guess because you were the prince and felt entitled."

"Fuck you, Dee! Fuck you!" he shouted again, pulling back his right arm and fisting up his hand as though he was winding-up to punch her in the face, just as he had the only time she ever babysat for him.

At that moment Dee saw Bessie come into the kitchen behind Georgie. Her mother's eyes were fierce and angry. She raised her precious cane with its gold handle and that bottom bit that was iron or something strong and dangerous, the cane that she intended to give Georgie in her will, and just as it was about to come down hard on the back of Georgie's head, Dee shoved her brother to the side and shouted, "Stop, Bessie! Stop! Don't!"

Bessie looked confused and held the cane midair.

Georgie saw her and screamed, "Hey! What the hell!"

Bessie cowered back and lowered the cane but still kept that hard iron tip pointed toward Georgie's belly button.

"Who are you?" Bessie yelled. "And what are you doing in my house?"

"Bessie, it's Georgie. It's Georgie, Bessie. You can put the cane down. It's okay. Don't be afraid. It's Georgie."

He swiped the tip of cane away from his stomach, and forcefully took the weapon away from his mother.

"It's not Georgie," she cried. "It's a bad man. My Georgie's a sweet little boy."

Georgie, the bad man, gave Dee a look with one eyebrow raised.

"What the hell?" he said.

"I don't like that kinda ugly talk, Mister. You should leave now," Bessie said. "I want my cane back. I want my cane back." Her face pinched up and she started to cry.

Georgie didn't give her the cane. Instead he backed away from the crazy woman.

"Bessie, do you know who I am?" Dee asked.

"Don't be silly." Bessie wiped her eyes with the backs of both hands. "Of course, I know who you are. You're Dee. You're my very best friend in the whole world, and this bad man was going to hurt you."

Dee stood motionless absorbing Bessie's words. *Best friend*, now that was lovely. She liked it. It was so much better than being the housekeeper.

"Bessie, I think you're still sleepy, let's go back and finish your nap, okay."

"I want my cane back."

Dee took the cane from Georgie and put it in her mother's hand.

"Are you sure this man isn't going to hurt you?"

"I'm sure."

She took Bessie by the arm and walked her back to the living room.

"After I lay down, Dee, you keep the cane with you, just in case he's up to no good."

"I will."

"Are you really-really sure you'll be safe?"

Dee nodded. After she got Bessie cozy on the couch, she gently patted her forehead and said, "Close your eyes now. It was just a bad dream. Close your eyes and go back to sleep."

Bessie closed her eyes for a second and then they popped back open, "I was dreaming?"

"Yep, now just relax and think of nice things, yellow roses and butterflies and red birds, think of good things and finish your nap."

Bessie closed her eyes and had a slight smile as she looked at the darkness of her lids and searched for pretty things. Dee went back to the kitchen.

"She's loony tunes," Georgie said in a coarse whisper.

"Keep your voice down. You'll scare her again."

She ran another glass of water. Counted to ten. Took a sip, then headed out the side door.

"Come outside," she whispered. "Let's be quiet so she can go back to sleep."

They stood on the back porch.

"I know this door was locked," she said.

He grinned. He stood there as smug as a child with lipstick on his face, claiming someone else got into his mother's makeup. Then the grin turned into a dark slit. He raged. "Jesus! She's dangerous. She should be in a nursing home. Jesus! She should be put away."

"You still have a key to the house? Forty years later?"

"I have my ways." Arrogant. Smug. Normal Georgie.

"Yeah, wise guy. I have ways too. I'm calling a locksmith."

"Lock me out, see what I care."

"You're dangerous. You were going to hit me before she came in the kitchen."

"Bullshit."

He was all bluster, standing there with his hands on his hips. Tough guy, but shaken, realizing he could have been lying dead on the kitchen floor with his head cracked open.

"You scared her. You scared me. She was half awake. She was protecting me. You scared her." She felt her hands shaking. She felt sick to her stomach. Why did being around him always make her feel ill?

"And she's not going to any damn nursing home. You said Dad beat you, well, he only spanked you that one time." She thought about how she hadn't stopped her father when he took off his belt and actually hit eight-year-old Georgie twice. Had she redeemed herself by stopping Bessie from hitting her brother or even killing him?

"Not true," he said, "You don't know everything."

There was something in the way he said it, a tone as petulant as his eight-year-old self, and she knew he was lying. One time. There was just that one time when her father took her brother "to the woodshed" and belted him twice.

All her life she had felt she was second fiddle to her mother's precious little prince, and meanwhile her brother felt neglected by their father. They were a dysfunctional family.

"He locked me in the coal bin, and you locked me in the bathroom."

"No, you hid in the coal bin after you destroyed Dad's fishing lures. And when I babysat for you, you locked the bathroom door and went out the window."

Someone was crazy around here and she was sure it wasn't her.

"How come Joey's truck was in the driveway?"

"We've been having hot sex," she said. A lie, they'd been having hot coffee...that's it, and in the company of her mother.

"Fat chance," he said and snickered. "I just can't see him being interested in you. I mean, have you looked in the mirror lately...or ever, actually?" He sneered and shook his head. "Ha! Hardly likely," he added. "So why was he really here?"

She decided that it was really okay if she hated her brother. She was sorry that he felt neglected by their father, but really, he was vile.

"He and several other contractors gave me quotes on the roof," another lie, but why not, and it would protect Zita. She wished for her sister-in-law to escape this nasty man. "And actually it's none of your damn business. You said, 'deal with it,' when I asked for your help with the roof. So that's what I'm doing. And by the way, if you're in the neighborhood spying on the house, why aren't you visiting your mother?"

"I'm not spying on the frigging house. I just happened to go by the side street."

"This is nowhere near either your house or your office."

"I have a client buying a house in the area."

"Yeah, right. Well, whatever, client or spy, your mother would love to see you more often."

"Why should I stop in here? You never make me feel welcome."

"What? That's not true. You stop in once a year, if that, I don't have the opportunity to make you feel unwelcome."

"You poured coffee on me."

"I thought you had hold of the cup."

He snickered then, "You and Joe Spinelli, Ha! Fat chance of that, in your dreams maybe. Ha."

She stared at him for a moment, then added, "By the way, Georgie, you should really take care of all those hairs growing out of your nose, or are you into that sloppy old man look?"

His hand went up to his nostrils.

"And now you can leave," she said. "Three taps and you're out." She tapped the dangerous tip of the cane hard on the concrete porch.

"One."

The cane hit the concrete again. Metal on concrete. Smack. A good sound.

"Two."

He shook his head with a look of disgust on his ugly, poorly groomed face and left.

When he was gone, she examined the lock on the side door and discovered it could be opened with a credit card. She used the wall phone in the kitchen to talk to a locksmith about coming out to put deadbolt locks on all the outside doors, and then she put Bessie's cane back in its usual spot leaning beside the couch during naptime.

When Bessie woke up an hour later, she told Dee about a very bad dream she had, and how this bad man had come into their kitchen and snatched her cane right out of her hands.

Dee loaded her mother up in the car and they went shopping for a cell phone.

*

She bought the new phone with the young salesman feigning great patience as he showed her how to use it, assumed she was an old woman (she was) and probably very dense about computers (she wasn't).

When they got home she searched for Zita's cell phone number. She remembered putting it in her shirt pocket. But then she had washed the shirt. She went to her room and found the folded paper still in the pocket— it was very clean. The numbers were so faint that she wasn't sure if the six was an eight, or the three was a five.

She had Joe Spinelli's business card, so his phone number was the first she entered in contacts. As she called him an erotic shutter ran through her body. The phone rang three times, and as it rang, she wondered if she'd hang up like a teenager when she heard his voice.

Finally, he said, "Hi, This is Joe,"

She said, "Hi..." but before she got another word out, he said, "Leave a message after the tone."

She waited for the tone, and then said, "Hi, Joey, this is Dee. I need to call Zita, but I washed..." then the phone beeped. She didn't speak fast enough.

She called the number again and repeated the message, and got as far as "washed" again before she was cut off.

She poured herself a cup of coffee, took a sip, paced the kitchen a little, then was going to try again, only this time she'd start with "washed."

The new phone rang, and she wasn't quite sure what to push, but it must've been right, because Joey was saying, "So what did you wash?"

"You're the first call on my new phone."

"I'm honored."

A ripple of giddiness ran through her. *He's honored, ha! So there, Georgie.*

Then she remembered why she was calling, "Joey, Zita gave me her cell number and I need to call her, but I accidently washed the number. Do you have it?"

He gave her the number and then asked if he could come by the next day and get the tarp on the roof, since rain was expected later in the week. The call was brief, no mention of coffee or anything personal. He was obviously busy. She pushed Georgie's comment—fat chance he's actually interested in you—out of her head. Fat chance. She wasn't going to be insecure. Joey was busy. Yeah, that was it. He was really busy.

*

Zita answered her phone on the first ring. She just listened as Dee told her about Georgie coming to the house, and how she lied and told him that she found the IOU and gave it to her lawyer. Then Dee said, "He's there, isn't he."

"Oh sure," Zita said, and laughed. "Can I call you back tomorrow, Lucille?"

"Yes," Dee said.

27. TARP

"A bird has a nest, man has a home."
Polish Proverb

"Dee, just so's you know, I think we have a bunch of woodpeckers on the roof."

"It's the roofers nailing down the tarp," Dee said

Two stories up from the kitchen, the muffled tapping could have been pecking. Two men were on the roof—neither was Joe Spinelli. She could feel insecure—was Georgie right? Joey couldn't be interested in her. Joey sent his guys, he was too busy to come. She was too...too...not enough. *No, don't do that to yourself. Joey's actually busy. Really.* Then in her head, Georgie snickered and said, Joey? Interested in you, fat chance.

"Tell me again, Dee, why are they doing that?" Bessie said. The perplexed look on her face was sincere.

"We have a leaky roof," Dee said, but her thoughts said, *do not be insecure...he's busy.*

She felt no impatience with Bessie's question. When Bessie had told Georgie that Dee was her best friend—it did something to her. Tenderized her, maybe.

Joey Spinelli hanging around was undoubtedly part of her good mood. But it bugged her that having coffee with him could have so much power over her emotions, so much power to change Bessie's redundancy into...into nothing, nothing to be irritated by, nothing more than a moment that passed before another moment came along. Why couldn't she be this patient before he came around? Or had she been patient? She remembered feeling so irritated, so frazzled sometimes that she wanted to scream. But had she shown it? She hoped not. A part of her still wanted to be that Dee that she imagined as a young girl. Dee: the Red Cross nurse, helping people with her kind and gentle ways. The white tent with the red plus sign on the roof had never been in her life, only in her imagination. The young soldiers that she would have helped never existed. Instead she had an ancient mother—trying her patience, but needing her just as much as a young man shot full of shrapnel.

"Is that man going to come have coffee with us today, Dee?" Bessie asked, "What's his name again?"

"Not today, Bessie. He's working at another house. His name is Joseph Spinelli."

"Spinelli," Bessie frowned, "I think that's Italian." She shook her head. "Don't you go getting too interested in him, Dee," she added. Then in a conspiratorial whisper, she said, "He's I-t-a-l-i-a-n." She spelled it out like a word you should avoid speaking out loud.

Just days ago, Bessie had approved of Joey.

"What's wrong with being Italian?" Dee asked.

"Mmm, you know, Dee." Bessie said, and wagged her finger at her daughter.

"No, actually I don't. Tell me," Dee said.

"They aren't of us."

"Are you saying you think they're less than you? Inferior?"

"No, I never said less, they're just not the same as us. You should stick with your own kind."

"But, Bessie, then you miss out on so much. If you're only associating with people just like you, it's...it's...it's like inbreeding. It's not healthy."

Dee thought of a time when she was a teenager just arriving home from school. Her mother was gardening in the front yard, when a car pulled up and an Asian woman stuck her head out of the driver's side window and called out, "Do you know if the house two doors down has been rented?"

And Bessie, who had no idea that the neighbor's house was even for rent, said with great charm and sweetness, "Oh, I'm so sorry. It's already rented."

Asian: not of us. Italian: not of us. The Not of Us list could go on and on.

"You never objected to my marrying Sy," Dee said. "His mother was Jewish. His father was Irish Catholic."

"Well, Dee, how could I object? You didn't ask my opinion, you just ran off to some Justice of the Peace. I didn't even get to be there. Anyway, I didn't see that you had a lot of prospects to choose from. How could I object? I didn't want you to be an old maid."

"A fate worse than death?"

"Better to be married to someone, anyone. Beggars can't be choosers."

This could hurt her feelings. As a young woman—certainly not as beautiful as her mother, but certainly not as homely as her mother thought—she had never been a beggar. Introverted, a little shy, maybe, but boys had liked her okay. Her feelings weren't hurt, because her reality wasn't the same as her mother's perception of her reality. It was much better. And she was secure enough in that knowledge that she didn't need to explain or defend her life to Bessie. Had it been her father's love that saved her? Had he made what could have been a sad broken girl into a whole woman?

"So, that Joey person. I think he's okay for coffee, but you shouldn't get serious about him. He's not of us."

Not of us—and we're oh so special. He's not of our tribe or clan. Dee hoped Bessie's world was disappearing. The world was getting smaller and more crowded all the time. Racism and bigotry might eventually disappear just because all kinds of people were getting to know each other. Things could change from "Not of us," to "Us." The Democrats chose Obama to be their choice for President of the United States, and the message was hope.

Hope for future generations. Dee thought that was a good thing.

28. MOWED

"Don't waste too many stones on one bird."
Chinese Proverb

July 4th, 2008, slipped by them with nary a sparkler, no booming fireworks, no watermelon dripping from their chins, no hot dogs sizzling on a grill in the back yard, no flag clasped next to the front door. The Rah-Rah holiday slipped away, like holidays can when there are no children around to awe and impress—no little blond Robin flying around the yard and leaping fences in a single bound. Dee felt bereaved.

She heard a whirring sound in their front yard—a lawn mower. Had Zita sent a lawn service? How thoughtful. But at the same time she was a little embarrassed. Zita had certainly noticed the long grass. She had said to let her know if there was anything she could do to help, and then she saw the lawn and just called a lawn service to fix it.

Dee went out on the porch. There wasn't a lawn service truck with a flatbed for riding mowers in front of their house, instead she watched as the man from next door went back and forth pushing his own mower. *How kind*, she thought.

The mower sputtered and came to a stop, and she took that quiet moment to call out to him, "Oh, thank you. You have no idea how much this means to me."

He seemed to ignore her as he pulled the starter. Perhaps the mower noise had deafened him a bit. When it was running again, he glanced at her and coarsely snapped the backside of his hand toward her, like he was shooing away an irritating sweat bee. The dismissive hand gesture was accompanied with a scowl in her direction.

She was mortified, like some loser who couldn't take care of her own space on earth. To be fair, the house did look shameful. It could've been a place where drug addicts, or lazy people, or old people lived—and she didn't want to be any of those.

She should offer to pay him. She should reimburse him for his trouble. Would twenty-five dollars be enough? Would he take it, or slap away her hand as she reached out, the bills fluttering to the ground, the wind picking up just then, and her running after two tens and a five. But then she reminded herself that he had never been a friendly neighbor, never once exchanged pleasantries over the fence. He lived alone, and Bessie referred to him as Mr. Grouch.

She glanced down the street, wondering if anyone else had seen him blow her off as he continued the task.

He wasn't looking happy to be lending a helping mow. His heart wasn't filled with generosity.

Neighborhood lawns were decorated with political signs. Barack Obama was now the presumed Democratic nominee for President, and several signs for him were on the lawns of her white, affluent suburban neighborhood. The whole Democratic Party had picked a black man for president. There was hope. Hope that racism was fading from America. She wondered if she could get a sign too. And what would Bessie think? Bessie, who, when she saw Obama come on the television wondered how a "colored" man could even be considered for president?

It was interesting Dee thought, that politicians never choose green or yellow for their signs. Let's hear it or see it for the flag—red, white, and blue. Rah. Rah. Their affluent suburban block only had one red, white, and blue lawn sign for John McCain. The rest were all for Barack Obama. People were changing.

Curious, she looked toward Mr. Grouch's house— who would he be choosing to promote on his lawn—but she couldn't see beyond his perfectly groomed poodle cut bushes, so she stepped down two porch treads, and then she saw Mr. Grouch's lawn sign—*For Sale by Owner.*

He was staging the neighborhood.

"Ok, fine, I get it," she called out, although he didn't hear over the mower noise, and she went back in the house, no longer ashamed, maybe feeling a little smug. The lawn was getting mowed.

And his timing was perfect.

29. Two Other Women

"Every shot does not bring down a bird."
Dutch Proverb

Before she opened the front door, Dee stood still for a moment composing herself—taking some deep breathes. Inhale. Exhale. Inhale. She could hear the two women on the porch talking together. They were unaware that she was cowering behind the door.

"Now here's what to watch for, Marnie," one voice said. "Does the mother flinch when the daughter comes near? Can you sense any fear on her part?"

Dee opened the door.

One of the women on the front porch was probably forty-something, eyes snappy and alert, a smile well practiced and warm—sincere, but well practiced. The other woman was the taller of the two—fresh-faced and eager as a puppy, ready to jump up and lick your face. They seemed pleasant and yet Dee was terrified. She was fully prepared for them, anyway, at least as much as possible, and yet her heart was racing. She had been forewarned, and yet her palms were sweaty. Bessie was lucid, and yet she couldn't trust what might come out of her mother's mouth.

How could Georgie do this? He was back at his games, but now he was playing dirtier. This was worse than trying to sue for his share of the estate, or having Bessie sign a blank sheet of paper, or breaking into the house when he thought they weren't home.

It wasn't chess he was playing. It was strip poker. He had stripped away all decency with his latest move.

"Are you Mrs. Chope?" the older of the two women asked. "We talked on the phone, I'm Harriet Manning from the Department of Human Services, Adult Protective Services. And this is our intern, Marnie McCormick." She stuck out her hand. Dee quickly brushed her sweaty palm against her slacks before shaking hands.

"Good morning," Dee said. "Come in."

*

She'd been warned days ago that Adult Protective Services would be calling or showing up, and she'd sprinted into action.

Every morning Bessie got a bath, at first squawking about it, then getting to like it. Bessie loved the attention, the warm water, the bubbling up of her hair. She liked the way Dee held her gently while she stretched back into the water to get rinsed. Dee poured a plastic cup of water carefully, so as not to get shampoo in Bessie's eyes, then washed her back. Bessie was the Princess farting in the bubbles. After the bath there was the combing and braiding of her long white hair.

After three days, Bessie woke up eager for her bath.

There was the house cleaning too. The kitchen floor got mopped—the linoleum was so worn between the sink and the stove that the dark gray backing was starting to show through, which made the floor look as if she hadn't cleaned it. She thought of putting down a throw rug to hide it, but then that could be a tripping hazard for an older person. All the furniture was dusted; all the floors were vacuumed. Everything was old and shabby, but it was as clean as old and shabby can get (which, truthfully, doesn't look all that clean).

She felt charged by her own fury—rage powered her scrubbing and rubbing and vacuuming. The hard work made her flex her muscles and feel in command. It was just housework, things she might normally do on a weekly or biweekly or triweekly basis, but with indignation powering her, it was something else. It was invigorating—expending more energy seemed to give Dee more energy. That's what she felt as she worked, but when she collapsed into a chair, the sick fear came back.

She told herself she could beat Georgie at this game, repeated it over and over to herself—trying to believe it.

*

Dee had an ally—Zita.

As their phone conversations became more frequent, Zita told Dee that they should both be removing any evidence of their communication. Zita told Dee to go to "Recents" on her cell phone and delete her phone number after each time they spoke—just in case Georgie got hold of either of their phones. In her phone's address book Dee changed Zita's name to Lucy Bell, with no address or email. Dee became Margaret Smith in Zita's phone. Zita could never come to Dee's house by herself, just in case Georgie was doing neighborhood surveillance.

Zita had overheard him on a call to social services. Dumb man, he always used the speaker on his phone (so he could strut around booming at the small rectangle on his desk, or maybe so the cell phone wouldn't mess up his hair). Anyway, she had come into his den as he was telling someone that he thought his mother was in danger. He saw Zita, his presumed ally, and put his finger to his lips to shush her. So she sat on a chair and listened as he ranted on about his mother smelling bad and having bruises on her arm and how he thought she wasn't getting enough to eat and what she did get to eat wasn't fresh—words like stale and dented cans flew out of his mouth.

"I'm very, very frightened for my mother's safety," he said.

The woman on the phone asked if his mother had seen a doctor or gone to an emergency room, since Social Services required a mandated report from a doctor on any physical abuse.

"What?"

"Well, could you take her to your family doctor?"

"No. My sister has changed the locks on the house and she won't let me in. She doesn't smell clean."

"Your sister?"

"No, my mother!" Suddenly he was shouting at the woman and sounding hysterical. "Who cares what my sister smells like? I'm deeply concerned about the situation. I think my mother should be in a nursing home and my sister should be arrested." Then he grinned at Zita, smug in his performance.

That outburst brought about questions from the Adult Protective Services lady about inheritance and the conditions of the home where his mother lived. When he described the area where the Ellison house was the voice on the phone said slow and drawn out, "Mmm, I see." Probably impressed. A hoity-toity neighborhood. High-falutin. The interview had gone on with several more questions on finances. Georgie looked at Zita, shook his head and shrugged like *why do they want to know that?*

When he got off the phone, he told his wife, "You know, people in nursing homes don't live long."

He obviously had forgotten about Bessie's brother Rob who thrived in a nursing home for ten years.

*

Dee had gotten the call from Social Services on the kitchen wall phone (the landline—the only number

Georgie had for her). The social worker said that she understood that Bessie had dementia and wondered what time of day would be the best to interview her. Lucid. Bessie should be at her most lucid.

The women from social services arrived at 11:00 a.m., which meant that Dee had time to get Bessie cleaned up with her hair smelling sweet and fresh. Dee (afraid that Bessie might suddenly accuse her of starving her to death) had set her up with graham crackers and a glass of milk for dunking. Messy, but it made her happy.

Bessie was in full charm and mental wellbeing when they arrived.

Dee brought the two women into the scrubbed kitchen, introduced them to Bessie, and offered them coffee, which they both accepted. Bessie offered to share her graham crackers. After the usual niceties, Marnie, the intern, shuffled her papers and asked questions. When she asked Bessie where do you bathe, Bessie nearly swooned. "I have a nice bath every single morning, and Dee washes my hair. Just so's you know, she's very good to me." She reached out then and patted Dee's hand. "She's gentle. Sometimes it's hard to get up out of the tub, because my knees are old. But she helps me."

Bessie obviously liked Dee caring for her, and didn't flinch at her touch—Dee felt a *whew* of relief.

"And how are you physically, Mrs. Ellison? I see you use a cane."

"I use it, but just so's you know, I don't really need it. It feels nice in my hand. And it reminds me of my father. He used it all the time when he was older."

"Have you ever felt threatened or afraid in the house?"

"Sometimes I have scary dreams," Bessie said.

"Oh, dear. What do you dream about?"

"Well, when I wake up, I can never remember my dreams. When I was a little girl I once dreamt I was walking down a dirt road and all of a sudden a hand shot up out of the dirt and chased me. It swatted at me with a stick. Just so's you know, that was the most scariest dream."

"You don't remember recent bad dreams."

"I can't. When I wake up, they're gone. Poof."

"That's okay, hardly anyone remembers their dreams. So where do you sleep, Bessie?"

"I have a nap in the living room, but my bedroom is upstairs.

"Are you able to go up and down the stairs safely?"

"I do. Do you want me to show you?" Bessie said, getting out of her chair before Marnie answered.

So Bessie went up the stairs on all fours with Dee following her, and then she sat her way back down the steps on her butt, and at the bottom Dee helped her stand upright.

"We recommend a hand rail on each side of the steps for added safety, but it seems your method of going up and down would make that unnecessary. Although, you might consider adding one anyway."

Back in the kitchen, Marnie, the young one, asked, "Have you ever gotten bruised or harmed in any way?"

"Not that I can think of," Bessie said. "No, actually, I did knock my arm against the door jamb one day, it really hurt, and it made a purple bruise.

"And you did that yourself?"

"I think old people take a long time to mend. Later it turned green. It was very ugly. I've been being more careful, watching where I'm going. But sometimes I forget. And you know, sometimes I'll just bump my hand a tiny bit and I get an ugly spot, like blood under my skin. Like this." She held out her hand and pointed at a purple blotch.

The two women separated Bessie and Dee; Marnie continuing to talk to Bessie in the kitchen, while Harriet went into the living room with Dee.

Dee tried to stay calm and chipper, but was afraid of what Bessie might say? That Dee starved her? She certainly didn't look starved. She had some good padding.

Harriet Manning asked, "So, Mrs. Chope, how long have you been caring for your mother?"

"Since my father died about ten years ago. You can call me Dee."

She was trying hard not to seem distracted, but couldn't help feeling anxious about the conversation in the kitchen. What was Bessie saying to Marnie?

"And what do you do besides care for your mother?"

"Well that's pretty much full time. She can't be left alone. She wanders."

"Do you get frustrated with her? Caregiving 24/7 can be exhausting. How do you handle it?"

"Years ago I was in a bad car accident, and afterward Bessie took care of me. She was patient. I remind myself of that when I feel irritable."

"But do you have any time for yourself?"

"When she naps, I like to sketch the birds outside the window and I read."

"Oh, so what are you reading lately?" Chatty. Friendly.

"Huh, reading? Oh, yeah, just old stuff. Library books. *One Flew Over the Cuckoo's Nest, Bird Man of Alcatraz* most recently."

"Hmm," Harriet said. "Both are about being confined."

She hadn't been writing anything down. Just talking like an old friend would that you hadn't seen in years—catching up.

"I can see how much you care for your mother. Also, I'm very aware of the affection between you. But I have to say I'm concerned about you. Do you know about AAA?"

"Car insurance?"

Harriet smiled. "No. The Area Agency on Aging. They might give you some relief. There are support groups, also you might check out adult day care for Bessie

once a week or at least every so often, that might give you
a break."

When the interview was over, Bessie sat on her green
plastic chair on the front porch, while Dee walked the
two women out to their car.

"I know that my brother reported us." Dee said. "He
thinks that Bessie should be in a nursing home. He thinks
that would shorten her life. He's very anxious to get his
inheritance."

Harriet Manning said. "You know, I've had a lot of
years experience at this. There are signs you pick up on. I
thought it would be an opportunity to bring Marnie out
on an easy case. We probably wouldn't have come out on
this one, but our interns need a chance to get real world
experience. I'll send a report back to your brother that his
concerns are unsubstantiated and that will close the case."

Harriet Manning stopped and stood still a moment.
"This happens in families, you know. Don't you worry, I
think your mother is doing fine. She's lucky to have you
caring for her. But if it ever gets to be too much for you,
or if I can be a service in any way, please don't hesitate to
call. I did give you my card, didn't I?"

"Yes." Dee patted her pocket.

*

As the car drove away down the street, she said out loud,
"If it's strip poker you're playing, Georgie, you just lost
your pants."

30. THE R BOOK

*"The bird hunting the locust
is unaware of the hawk hunting him."*
Portuguese Proverb

There's anonymity in being old. You can go into the grocery store without makeup and nobody cares, nobody sees you unless you're really outrageous; unless you're wearing a fuchsia feather boa; unless you're sockless in sandals in the middle of a blizzard; or unless you're making birdcalls at the top of your lungs.

She hadn't heard from Joey Spinelli—not since before Georgie broke in—and all the hurt teenage girl insecurities were swirling in Dee's head. Georgie was right. Why would someone like Joe Spinelli be interested in her? She was never pretty, and now she had reached beyond being plain into being old and invisible. How could she have imagined that he was interested in her?

Bessie was napping, and Dee was drawing half-heartedly in her father's study, actually just listlessly scribbling. She was bored with the drawings, there were no interesting bird competitions going on outside the window. She sighed and glanced around the room at the bookshelves that she should probably dust. She stood up and went to the shelves, examined—one by one—the spines of the books her father had read. She ran her finger along their edges and could see her father in this room with his glasses sliding off the end of his nose, using two fingers on the bridge to push them back up, searching out some treasure buried in the mahogany— Thoreau, Poe, Emerson, Stevenson, all the classics she read in high school. Then, there were his mysteries—a whole shelf of Elmore Leonard. Her tracing finger came to the encyclopedias and landed on the R volume. R had been the book that always made her feel better. She pulled the book from its cramped grip between the PQ and S volumes and took it to the desk. She would reread the Eleanor Roosevelt entry; when she was young Eleanor soothed her; Eleanor reminded her that there were more important things than being pretty, like kindness and concern for others. When she opened the book she wasn't surprised that the book—that she'd trained over several teenaged years to open to a specific page—fell open to the Eleanor Roosevelt entry.

But no, the book opened to Eleanor because there were two sheets of neatly folded paper stuck between the pages. Could she have left some note in the book? Maybe one of her letters to Grandma Eleanor?

She carefully opened the heavier sheet of paper, expecting to see her own handwriting or a drawing.

Instead it was a legal looking document with the embossed stamp of a notary. She read the date and then the words:

> *October, 13, 1997.*
>
> *George Ellison agrees to repay a loan of $100,000 to his father, Jack Ellison, in the amount of $1,000 per month until the loan is repaid in full. If there is still debt owed when Jack Ellison is deceased, the payment must be made to Bessie Ellison, if she is deceased the payment must go to his sister Delores Ellison Chope.*

Both parties and the notary had signed the agreement. The second sheet in the book was lined notebook paper with blue inked vertical lines making it a chart. Handwritten at the top of the left column was DATE, beneath it numbers: 1/1/1998 then 2/1/1998 and so on. Jack had given Georgie a two and a half month grace period before payments were scheduled to begin. The second column was headed—AMOUNT PAID. That column had notes her father had written. *Nothing!* After each date for a year he had written *"Nothing!"* Then his ulcer blew up. The rest of the column was blank. There was no indication that Jack was charging Georgie any interest to be paid on this loan—a loan that necessitated Jack taking out a second mortgage on the house, and paying the interest himself. How much of the stress that caused the bleeding ulcer had come from Georgie's big loan?

When she told Georgie she had found the IOU, could he tell she was lying? The IOU included payment to her, that had to have infuriated him, and maybe was part of the reason that he never paid their father back. If the point of asking to borrow money was really to test Jack's love and loyalty, then the plot had kicked back and smacked Georgie in the face. He was obviously jealous of his sister and his father made him agree to pay her.

Her father hid the IOU in the Roosevelt book—so he must have known—must have noticed the R volume coming and going from the shelf. He must have discovered that it spent time in her room all those years ago? Maybe he had looked at Eleanor Roosevelt just as she had? Maybe he'd seen a reflection of his daughter there? Had he observed how Bessie had rejected her as a child, and become more attentive? If he was loaning all this money to Georgie, maybe he didn't want Dee left out? Dee was living at home when the IOU was written. She was fully recovered from the accident and back to work. Or maybe Jack was just covering all the bases, making sure that Georgie's debt repayment wouldn't lapse if both parents were deceased.

When Bessie woke up from her nap, they went to see Ray Ridgewell. Dee had already told Georgie that she had taken the IOU to her lawyer, and now she did it.

31. UNDER WATER

"'I have' is a better bird than 'if I had'."
German Proverb

Summertime and the living is...not necessarily easy.

A bath every morning was getting old, even to Bessie, so they made an agreement between themselves— a bath every other day should keep Social Services away, but then they lost track and it was three days before another bath, and then Bessie wasn't in the mood.

"But your hair is starting to look stringy," Dee said, and continued running the bath water.

She sniffed Bessie's head, "And you don't smell like a flower."

"Maybe I do smell like a flower, like a marigold maybe?" Then Bessie laughed—a cackle like a wicked witch in a Disney movie.

Here was her mother—a dedicated groomer all her life—and she really didn't care anymore.

"You must think I'm a duck or something," Bessie said. "I don't like being in the water."

"I always thought you were a swan."

Bessie grinned.

"But what if someone from Adult Protective Services comes back and smells your head and says you have to go live in a nursing home?"

"Okay. Call her up. I'll go pack my suitcase."

Bessie headed back toward her bedroom.

"Just so's you know, I don't want to take a bath ever anymore. Just so's you know, I don't want to get all wet and soggy."

"Okay. Fine with me, I'll take the bath."

Dee stripped and got into the tub. She settled back in the warmth of the water, closed her eyes and let the water fill her ears so sound was muffled like she was deep in the ocean, scuba diving, maybe. Then she thought about Joey, imagined him in the bathroom with her, imagined him leaning over the tub and rubbing a soapy hand on her breasts, she closed her eyes, her lips puckered to accept his kiss.

An actual hand touched her shoulder, and she burst up from the water.

"Did I scare you, Dee?" Bessie said. "I'm sorry."

"It's okay."

"Do you want me to wash your back?"

"No," Dee said, touched that Bessie offered. "It'd be too hard on your knees to kneel by the tub, besides, I thought you were packing."

"I was, but I can't remember if I have a suitcase, and then your little phone rang and I didn't know how to answer it, and then a minute later the phone in my bedroom rang, and it was a man wanting you, Dee. And I told him you were in the bathtub and to call back later. I think he was selling something."

"Did it sound like Joey?"

"Who's Joey?"

"Never mind."

*

Clean, dry, dressed, hair brushed and blown—she waited. She made them breakfast and waited for the phone to ring. She found Bessie's suitcase, and Bessie wondered why she needed a suitcase. Hours passed and she made lunch.

It was probably one of those robocalls, where they tell you that there's no problem with your credit card, but if you're interested in a lower interest rate....blah, blah, blah. Or maybe it had been someone wanting her to vote for someone.

But it hadn't been Joey. Probably not. Since she was new to the whole cell phone thing, it never occurred to her that she could just look at the phone to see who called.

She might need a dose of Eleanor Roosevelt again.

She felt stupid for caring so much, for wanting him to call. She went out on the porch and wished she still had cigarettes. Just one long deeply inhaled drag.

So, you know how it works—just when she gave up waiting, the phone rang and his name came up on the screen of her new cell phone. She let it ring twice, because she didn't want to seem too eager or needy.

He called to invite her out to dinner. Friday night. A date. His daughter-in-law would come sit with Bessie.

32. WHITE GLOVES

"Every bird needs its own feathers."
Danish Proverb

She'd stalled too long. It was Friday morning and she still hadn't told Bessie about her date. But maybe it was better waiting until the last minute, that meant there was less time for Bessie to fuss at her, or say something bad about Italians, or make her feel more insecure than she already did.

She poured her mother a cup of coffee, handed it to her and just blurted it out, "I have a date tonight."

"A date?"

"A date."

Bessie laughed and said, "School girls have dates. You can't have a date. Whose wanting to date you anyway? The milkman?"

"We don't have a damn milkman, Bessie."

"I heard that swear word, Dee."

"Okay. Sorry," she said. She took a deep breath, preparing herself. Decided not to mention Joey's last name. "Remember Joey, the contractor, the one who's going to fix our leaking roof. He had coffee with us. You liked him. Remember that?"

"No."

"He's very nice. Funny. He's invited me out to dinner with him." She felt like a kid, expected the next words out of her mouth to be, *Can I go, Mama. Please let me go.* She clamped her lips together instead.

"But, Dee, if you leave, I'll be all alone. Are you going to leave me here all by myself? I'll be afraid."

She sat down next to Bessie at the kitchen table, and said softly, "He's bringing his daughter-in-law to sit with you, and keep you company. I'll fix your dinner early, so you'll be all set."

"Do I know this person, this daughter-in-law person?"

"You'll meet her tonight. I'm sure she's nice. You'll be fine. You can watch TV with her."

"I'm not happy," Bessie whispered.

"I'm sorry."

"What if you like being away from me and don't come back? Georgie never calls or visits. It hurts me, you know, that he doesn't care about me. If you left me, I wouldn't have anyone at all. I'd be abandoned."

"Of course, I'll be back. I'd never abandon you. You can count on me. Haven't I always been here with you? Rain or shine."

Bessie rattled her spoon around in her coffee cup, then she gave Dee a wane smile. "You should have a date.

It'd be good for you. Maybe you'd stop being so grouchy."

"I'm not grouchy."

"Yes, you are, and you say bad words. You shouldn't say any ugly words on this date. Men don't like women who swear."

"Okay."

"And you should do something with your hair. And have you thought about what you're going to wear."

Had she thought about it? For days she had been pushing things around in her closet. Pulling out. Trying on. Taking off. Putting back.

"I was thinking that pink blouse Robin gave me for my birthday, and black slacks."

"Not a dress? Men like ladies in dresses."

"And white gloves?"

"Oh, yes. White gloves and a dress. Ha, just so's you know, Dee, I know that glove part was sarcastic."

Dee laughed.

"Yeah, you're right. It was."

"Let's go upstairs and see if I have something you could wear. I do have some very nice gloves."

Bessie got up, leaving her coffee behind and headed for the stairs.

"And you should go somewhere, a saloon and have a real person do your hair," Bessie added.

Dee laughed. "Ha, I'll have a beer and a haircut please. You mean salon, Bessie. And by the way, I'm a real person. I like to do my own hair. I don't like how you go to a salon where they make women my age look like old ladies. Maybe they'd dye my hair blue."

"You'd look nice with blue hair. It'd go with your eyes."

They both laughed and went upstairs to look for Bessie's gloves.

33. FISH ON FRIDAY

"He has gone in pursuit
of the birds of the sea."
Xhosa Proverb

Joey's daughter-in-law was a black woman, and Dee felt a moment of stress when she saw her standing at the front door with Joey. What would Bessie say or do? Would she be rude, refuse the woman's company? Also, if Bessie was cruel to Joey's daughter-in-law would it reflect back on Dee. But on the other hand, if Bessie was anything at all, she was gracious. She was always proper to peoples' faces.

"Come in, come in," Dee said, holding the door wide.

Inside, Joey said, "This is my daughter-in-law, Theresa."

"It's so nice to meet you," Dee said. "And so kind of you to sit with Bessie."

"Oh, I'm happy to do it. We've all been thinking that it's way past time Papa Joe got out and had some fun. Did he tell you that I work in a nursing home? I get along great with older folks."

"Actually, she's the director there," Joey said.

Bessie came into the front hall then, and Theresa took Bessie's hand in both of hers and told her how happy she was to meet her, and what a nice time they'd have together.

Bessie's eyes went wide open with alarm; Dee didn't think the others saw it, but she did. Bessie nodded a hello, but didn't speak.

"Would anyone like a glass of wine or cup of coffee before we go?" Dee asked. Stall a bit, let Bessie get comfortable. She hadn't said a word yet.

Theresa said, "Oh, now don't you worry, Dee, Bessie and I are going to be just fine, why don't you two just get on with your evening." She took a bag from Joey that Dee hadn't noticed before, and added, "We brought ice cream."

"I like ice cream," Bessie said.

"So let's take this to the kitchen, Bessie. Lead the way. Have you had your dinner yet?"

As Bessie headed toward the kitchen, Theresa turned to Dee and Joey and said, "Scat, you two. Bessie and I are going to have a wonderful time."

*

She had expected him to pick her up in his pickup, but he had a car. He opened the door for her and she felt like a woman on a real date, maybe in the nineteen-fifties, kinda nice.

When he got in on his side and was set to drive off she pulled Bessie's white gloves out of her purse.

"Bessie thought I should wear these."

He laughed.

"Are your hands cold? It's supposed to get all the way down to 70 degrees tonight. Of course, that's not taking into consideration the wind chill factor."

"I'm getting goose bumps already."

"You look very pretty," he said, and took her hand. "I don't think you'll need gloves, your hand is nice and warm."

She felt herself glow as pink and pretty as her pink blouse.

He took I-696 (locally referred to as the Detroit Autobahn, because there's a tendency to speed) to the east side to a restaurant in St. Clair Shores, where they sat outside on a deck looking out at the lake. Bits of white light sparkled on the ripples of water, shades of blue gray faded all the way to the horizon line. No land in sight. Canada was too far south of them to be visible. They inhaled lake scents—water, seaweed, tanning products on nearby people. They had fish and chips, while watching a particular sea gull strut around between tables in search of its own dinner out.

They talked about their kids and grandkids. He also had a son and daughter and three grandchildren. They matched.

And then he confessed that this was not only their first date but a celebration of sorts. He told her he had just sold his business. He was sixty-seven. Time to retire and have some fun. Climbing around on roofs wasn't so exciting anymore. It hurt his knees.

"At my age you don't bounce when you fall off a roof."

"Did you ever bounce?" she asked.

"Oh, sure," he said, and laughed.

He told her that the new company (actually an old company) that bought him out would finish the roof on her house.

After their dinner, he drove along Lake Shore Drive and parked at the Grosse Pointe War Memorial. They walked through the garden holding hands and looking out at Lake St. Clair. He kissed her. At such an intimate moment she scolded herself for wondering if he'd stood on his tiptoes? It didn't seem like he was shorter at all. But why think about height when soft, sweet lips are touching yours? Good kisser. Moist, soft lips. In her rapid fire kissing assessment she felt like Goldilocks judging his lip action? Not sloppy or too juicy. Not dry and scratchy. Just right. She stopped thinking. And he kissed her again more intently, sending a quiver though her. When he pulled away, she leaned forward to continue the kissing.

Summertime. Daylight savings. It was still light when he brought her home. They went inside and found Theresa and Bessie sitting close together on the couch and laughing hard at something on the TV. Theresa slapped her knee and hooted and then Bessie did the same.

"Wow," Dee said, but wasn't sure either of them heard her, so she shouted out, "Looks like you guys are having fun."

They glanced at her and quickly back at the TV. She and Joey exchanged grins.

"How about some decaf?" she asked.

He nodded and then went and sat in the living room.

When she came back with four cups of coffee on a tray there was a commercial break and she heard Joey telling them about their date.

A commercial for Obama came on the TV.

"Why are they still advertising?" Bessie said, "The election's over. McCain won. Just so's you know, that's seems so silly, putting ads on TV now. A waste of money."

"Bessie, the election isn't till November. It's just July," Dee said.

Joey said, "Well, maybe we're all just sick of all the commercials, so it feels like it should be over."

Theresa said, "You know, Bessie has been telling me all about growing up in Traverse City."

These are nice people, Dee decided. Joey justified Bessie's confusion and Theresa changed the subject.

Bessie might have been embarrassed, but if so, it passed quickly. She perked up, and said, "I was telling Theresa how my mother kept a big wheel of cheese in the cellar in Traverse City and how when I'd come home from school I'd sneak a slice. Sneaked food tastes best, but the problem is you have to eat it fast before someone comes along and catches you."

They all watched the TV for a while, Joey and Dee sneaking glances at each other.

When Joey and Theresa left (no last kisses involved, but fingertips touched) Bessie and Dee sat on the front porch in the dark.

"Well, did you have a nice time?" Bessie asked.

"Very nice. We had fish at a restaurant on Lake St. Clair. How about you? Did you have a good time?"

"She's very nice. After a while I forgot she was colored, but I forget things sometimes. But you know what was really good, Dee?"

"What?"

"She brought chocolate ice cream. My favorite."

"Could she come visit you again some time?"

"She was very nice, Dee. Just so's you know, I think you should get to know her. You'd like her. And yes, she should visit again. But next time we'll get the ice cream. Okay?"

34. HOME

"Each bird loves to hear himself sing."
Native American Arapaho Proverb

"I'm ready to go home now," Bessie said. She had gone to the front hall closet of the house she'd lived in for sixty-seven years and put on her wool winter coat.

"Where's home?" Dee asked.

Bessie didn't speak. Was she trying to remember where she had grown up? Moments passed, then looking puzzled, she said, "North, North from here, I think."

Dee was tired after a poor night's sleep. Too many sleepless minutes in bed replaying the conversation at dinner with Joey, trying to recall every word, and then many, many minutes remembering the kissing by the lake, then more minutes wondering if he was awake reliving their date too.

"Oh, Bessie," she said, hearing her own tired voice. "You *are* home, and it's a beautiful morning. It's too hot for that coat. July. It's July 25th. You don't need a coat."

"But, I want to go home and see my mother. I miss my mother. I think she misses me, too."

"Bessie, do you know who I am?"

Bessie looked insulted, clucked her tongue and shook her head, "You're Dee. You're my housekeeper. Don't you remember who you are? Are you going senile or something?"

"No, Bessie, I'm your daughter."

Bessie laughed at that one—a good joke. "Now you're being funny. I'm not even married yet. How could I have a daughter?"

Distract, divert, maneuver, sidestep, and agree with untruths—the mantra rang in Dee's head.

"Okay, then," Dee said, "I'm your housekeeper."

"I think you're my driver too. Will you take me home now."

"Okay," Dee said, "but take that coat off."

"I might get cold. I think it's cold in my mother's house. I better wear it. You know my house is almost at the top of the mitten. Michigan's a mitten. Did you know that? Only the bottom part is a mitten. The top is some other shape."

"How about you take off the coat and just carry it. I don't want you to have a heatstroke."

After she got Bessie belted into the car, Dee drove up and down blocks in the neighborhood, here and there pointing out someone's garden. As she talked sweetly to her mother, her impatience dissipated. She talked about the zinnias and yellow roses. She exclaimed over all the beautiful colors. At first Bessie clutched her wadded up coat to her chest and stared straight ahead, anxious to get home to see her mother, but gradually, particularly at the mention of roses, she turned her head to see.

"I wonder how they smell?" Dee said. "Do you like the smell of roses best or some other flower?"

"Lilacs smell the best," Bessie said. "One spring I had some lilac perfume on, and I was riding in the car with your father, and as we drove by some big bushes, he said, 'Just smell those lilacs'." Bessie laughed. "The car windows were closed! He was smelling me!"

They both laughed. Dee already knew this story, but the good thing was that Bessie remembered Jack. She remembered that she had been married and she that she had had a husband.

"Lilacs come out in the spring,' Bessie said. "So what smells best now are roses. I had beautiful roses in my garden. Remember that, Dee?"

Then Bessie asked, "Where are we going anyway? Costco?"

Dee said. "Traverse City."

Bessie looked at Dee as though she was losing it. "Traverse City? Why would you want to drive to Traverse City? That's where I grew up. It's too far a drive, Dee. I'd rather go home and have lunch."

When they were parked back in their own driveway, Dee suggested that they sit in the back yard to eat. The day was too beautiful to be cooped up in the house.

"Bologna sandwiches?" Bessie said, and clapped her hands together, the equivalent of the eager tail wagging of a puppy anticipating a treat.

"Peanut butter and jelly today. Okay?"

"Strawberry jelly? Put on real thick?"

"Yep."

Bessie smiled approval.

Dee walked Bessie around the house to the backyard. She put her palm on the yellow chair—it was comfortably warm. Sometimes the metal sitting in the sun would get so hot it would blister a bottom. It was still early, too soon for the chair to overheat, and really too soon for lunch, but she didn't care.

"Okay, Bessie, sit here, enjoy the sun on your face, while I go make our lunch."

Inside from the kitchen window, she could see the back of Bessie's chair. She thought she heard Bessie singing, and cranked open the window to listen. "Take me out to the ballgame," floated into the kitchen. Peanuts and Cracker Jacks and all the lines of the song never got mangled in Bessie's memory. But she stopped singing before getting to the final line, and Dee sang out the window, "For it's one, two, three strikes, you're out, at the old ball game."

She put on a fresh pot of coffee, and while she waited for it to complete it's dripping, she watched Bessie out the window, prepared to run out if Bessie got up and started walking off somewhere. Dee spread the jelly thick on Bessie's sandwich.

She called out the window, "I'm sorry it's taking so long for the coffee to get done."

Finally she poured two cups of coffee, Bessie's in her favorite radioactive red Fiestaware cup with half and half, and lots of sugar, and loaded it all on a tray.

35. NAP

"When the cage is ready, the bird has flown."
French Proverb

Bessie's eyes were shut. The sun on her face must feel good, because she had a slight smile. Napping.

Dee congratulated herself on a job well done. Bessie was calm again. Divert, distract, maneuver, and trick. It worked.

She set the tray on the sagging picnic table, and reached into her pocket for a cigarette. There weren't any, she'd quit weeks ago, right before Robin's visit, but hadn't gotten over the habit of reaching into her pocket. You don't want your young granddaughter to think bad habits are okay. Some days she didn't even think about smoking. She had weaned herself off. She smiled—something else to be glad about on this lovely day.

She'd had a date with Joey and it went so amazingly well, she couldn't find a thing not to like about him. There would be more dates, more kissing, she felt confident. And Bessie liked Theresa. Dee felt absolutely lucky.

Bessie shifted—slumped down more in her chair. Now she looked uncomfortable, like she'd get a crick in her neck. She should wake up anyway, while her coffee was still hot and before her sandwich dried out. She went over to her mother and touched her cheek, whispered, "Bessie, your lunch is here." Then she added with a musical tone, "Strawberry jelly."

Then Dee noticed that the black cane was abandoned on the grass. It was normally propped against the side of whatever chair Bessie sat on. It probably dropped when Bessie fell asleep.

She rubbed Bessie's shoulder and then knelt beside her—not thinking about her own knees or the effort it would take to get back up—looking up at her mother's translucent skin and baby fine long white hair. She took Bessie's cool hand, so cool on a warm day, and held it in hers and ran her fingertip along the raised blue veins and knotty joints, but Bessie didn't wake up.

Bessie's hand wasn't cold, just cool. Cooling down. The heat of her, the life of her, was gradually dissipating. Dee jumped up and ran into the house and picked up the receiver on the kitchen wall phone, completely forgetting that she had a cell phone in her pocket. She stopped. Didn't dial any number. She looked out into the backyard at her mother slumped in her chair. Should she call an ambulance? Maybe they could revive her?

But then they'd take her to Beaumont Hospital and hook her up to a machine to keep her alive. Next there'd be a nursing home with a vague smell of urine where Bessie would beg strangers to take her home as she rolled around in a wheelchair with her body slumped to one side.

Bessie didn't want any of that. She didn't want to be plugged in.

But maybe she was really just napping?

Dee went back outside, she pulled the other yellow chair up facing her mother. She took Bessie's hand and stroked her fingers. She said, "Bessie, are you still here. Wake up now."

Just minutes before, her mother had been singing. It would be the perfect way to go. Singing one minute and asleep forever the next. It was good, but too good to be true. A happy ending, but Dee didn't trust that it was real. Maybe it was her who was asleep. Maybe she was dreaming. She stood up and walked to the vegetable garden. Kicked at a clump of dirt. Saw the dust of it rise and fall. She wasn't dreaming. She heard a bird—a robin—whistling on the high wire at the back of their yard. She mimicked it and whistled back. He responded. She whistled again.

Then she walked back to Bessie and sat in the chair beside her. She took a bite of her peanut butter and jelly sandwich.

She said, "Hmm, Bessie, this is really good. Wake up, or you'll miss out." She slowly ate her sandwich. Then she drank her cup of coffee. The sun warmed her hair. It was a nice day.

"Bessie, if you don't wake up, I'm going to eat your sandwich."

And she did.

After each bite, she said, "See, Bessie, I'm eating your sandwich, you better wake up quick."

She finished both cups of coffee and waited for Bessie to wake up. Then she had to pee, so she went into the house. When she came back outside, Bessie still hadn't moved. And although she had never been much of a crier, tears ran down her cheeks. She took the tray with the empty cups into the kitchen and dialed 911.

*

At the suggestion of the policeman who came to the house, she called the funeral home that had taken care of her father. They were still in business and sent a hearse out to get Bessie. When everyone was gone she sat in the kitchen alone. The house was quiet as a rock. Strange. But as she sat in the silence, she heard the clock on the stove make a thin whirring sound, and at regular intervals it clicked. She'd never heard it before.

She'd need to call people.

She should call Georgie. Should. Should. Didn't.

She could picture him coming into the house carrying a clipboard to list the treasures he'd move to his lair. She wasn't ready to deal with him yet. She'd have to, but not yet.

It happened too fast. One minute Bessie wanted to go home, the next she was gone. It was hard to digest. Hard to believe. Hard. Just hard.

She didn't want to be in the house. So she left. She took her cell phone, sunglasses and purse and drove to a neighborhood park. The park was beside a school that was closed for the summer. Mothers pushed their children on swings. A skinny-armed kid swung his little body on the horizontal ladder. Others were sliding and climbing on an enormous sprawling green metal structure.

She sat and watched them and tried to figure out what she felt. It was too soon to know.

36. SHARING

*"The early bird may catch the worm,
but the second mouse gets the cheese."*
American Proverb

Dee called them all, there weren't that many. Amy cried and said they'd all come home. She tried to reach her son, Paul, and left a message with his squadron commander. Georgie said he'd be right over. Joey was sorry about Bessie, and said he'd come over that evening. Lawyer Ray gave his condolences.

She breathed in the heat of the afternoon—eighty degrees. She preferred the heat pulling into her nose to being inside. The house still had everything in it; it was all exactly the same, but it felt empty. Bessie was gone.

Georgie arrived first. He got out of his Cadillac, gingerly climbed the front steps and sat down beside Dee on the front porch.

He didn't ask what funeral home Bessie was at, or how she died, or if she'd called out his name in her last moment. He didn't say hello or how are you.

"I'll buy out your share of the house."

Was her brother a psychopath? After he broke into the house she thought that maybe he was a sociopath, so she had looked up sociopath and psychopath on WebMD. Psychopaths weren't necessarily serial killers. But they were without conscience. Georgie seemed to be without conscience—cunning, charming, calculating and determined to get what he wanted without being concerned with anyone else. So if you grow up with a sibling with serious mental problems, what does that do to your childhood? How are you formed (or warped) in that environment?

"Our mother just died and that's the first thing you say?"

"Yeah."

She felt like the front porch was a stage and this was all a play. Her next line should be, "Have you no shame, Sir? Have you no shame?" So she said it and he ignored it.

"My guy will come out and appraise the house. Man, this place is in bad shape. Not worth much in this condition."

She smiled. Did he even realize how transparent he was? Not worth much? Then why did he want it so badly?

"Still haven't fixed the roof, I see," he said.

"Nope."

"Bad roof depreciates the value."

The new owner of Joey's company would come get the tarps off the roof. And then it would be up to Georgie to deal with buckets and drips and a new roof.

"Bessie wanted you to have her cane," Dee said.

"You mean that black cane that she tried to kill me with?"

"That's the one."

"You take it. Why the hell would I want the thing?"

"Sentimental value. You can look at it and remember me saving your life."

She laughed.

He left.

37. GATHERING

"Every bird has a hawk above it."
Croatian proverb

The funeral was poorly attended, or rather, you could say it was an intimate affair: Dee, Georgie and Zita, Amy with her husband Matt and their three kids, Ray Ridgewell came with his wife, and Joey Spinelli brought his daughter-in-law Theresa. All the old friends and relatives, who had once known Bessie, had either died or forgotten her. She was her parents' youngest child. The last survivor—until she wasn't. Dee's son Paul had called and recounted how much he had loved his grandmother Bessie, but he was still stuck in Afghanistan and couldn't come home.

They had a small service at the funeral home. A rent-a-minister read a bible verse and then asked if anyone cared to speak. Georgie got up and read something he'd written on a yellow sheet of legal paper. He talked about his devotion to his mother, the best person he'd ever known. He got choked up and the minister patted his shoulder. Dee pinched Amy's baby finger and glanced at her daughter. Amy rolled her eyes.

Four-year old Robin wanted to speak, and they let her. She stood in front of the small group and said, "She was a good Bessie." Then she bowed and went back to her chair.

Amy shared childhood memories of her grandmother.

Dee sat.

Bessie had lived a long life, people took care of her—first her parents, her five older brothers in Traverse City, then Jack, and then Dee. The first years of Bessie's life she had been privileged, wealthy, wanting for nothing, or at least nothing that she had thought to want. The last years of her life she had been poor—not deep poor with rats and a cold furnace in the house, cardboard in the windows and dumpster dive dinners. Poor relative to her past. Frill-less. Basic. Not sad or uncomfortable, but careful, conscious—directed and overseen by her daughter.

Everyone was invited back to the house for lunch. Amy had ordered a spiral cut ham and all the usual fixings, potato salad, rye bread, baked beans, cheesecake and cookies. The usual wake or picnic food.

Dee sat on the couch and Amy came and cozied up beside her.

"How are you, Mom?"

How did she feel? "I feel like I just lost 135 pounds. Lighter. Like I can breathe easier."

Amy laughed. "Well, that's all good. Anyway, I think it's good. You're not getting anorexic are you?"

"Nope. But Amy, when you lose so much so fast you have all this excess skin hanging off your body. Skin you have to cram into your pants. Arm flab, like you can't even imagine, crowding the sleeves of your blouse."

"Come home with me, Mom. Come live with us."

"Thank you. I'm glad you want me. But, Amy, I think I have to get used to having all this loose skin first."

Amy begged Dee to come back to Wisconsin and live with them in the orchard. Robin even offered to share her pink bedroom with her. She told them both that she would surely come visit a lot, maybe spend a month in the summer there, but she didn't want to leave Detroit just yet.

Did Dee mourn her mother? Was she lonely, lost without someone to care for? Did she feel like she was supposed to feel sadder than she did? Did she feel guilty for not being sadder than she was? Not one tiny sliver. Which was what she told herself whenever she made herself a cup of coffee and still took down Bessie's radioactive red cup.

Was she calm and relieved? Could she acknowledge to herself that she had done her best caring for Bessie? Did a feeling of quiet peace enfold her? Did Einstein have wild eyebrows?

38. LOCATION, LOCATION

"The hunter in pursuit of an elephant
does not stop to throw stones at birds."
Ugandan Proverb

It all happened very quickly.

In the days following Bessie's death, Joey brought an appraiser friend of his to the house. The guy wrote out everything that was wrong, and everything that was right—location, location, location—and came up with an estimated value of the house. When Georgie's choice of appraiser came to the house, she showed him the other man's write-up. And after taking a very quick survey of the house, he said, "Yeah, that looks right," and wrote down his numbers but added a few dollars more to the value. Georgie didn't like either appraisers numbers, but lawyer Ray said, "tough."

Georgie backed down. He definitely wanted the house.

When Ray told Georgie he'd have to repay Dee the money he'd borrowed from his father, Georgie had a temper tantrum. "That's old news," he shouted. "There's nothing legally binding in that old IOU." In other words, *you can't make me, na na na.*

"It's legally notarized. A legal contract," Ray said.

"You can't prove that I didn't pay him back."

Ray held up the sheet of paper that Jack had created, the payment sheet, showing no payments.

"There's nothing legal about that."

Dee said, "Maybe I should just stay in the house. I could make monthly payments to you for your share, Georgie."

At that, Georgie sputtered some profanity under his breath and stomped out of Ray's office.

"Don't worry," Ray said. "He'll be back. He really wants the house."

"Do you think maybe he discovered a gold vein running though the old coal bin?" she said.

"Hmm, or maybe there's oil under the back yard."

The next day Georgie called Ray and agreed to pay Dee the loan money. That seemed too quick, too easy. Maybe there really was a vein of gold running through the basement. She didn't trust Georgie, and now he was complying. Why?

Ray said, "Just accept it. This is what you want. Right?"

It was. She wanted to fly the coup.

He met them at the title company's office for the closing and turned over two certified checks, one for Dee's share of the house and one for the debt. They signed papers. She gave him a set of keys to the new deadbolt locks.

"So what are you going to do with it?" she asked him.

He looked smug, "Do you know what property values are around here? I'll sink some money into the house...new kitchen with granite counters, stainless steel appliances, new roof, some paint. I'll make a fortune." He laughed. He was proud of how he had put one over on her. "Four times what I paid you! Including the damn IOU money."

"Funny, Georgie," she said, softly, "I have more, much more than I'll ever need. And no matter how much you have, you'll never have enough."

As she stood to leave, she patted his shoulder, and said nicely, "Well, good luck to you."

He gave her two weeks to move out.

She deposited Georgie's checks in the bank and called Zita.

"It's done," she said.

Zita's lawyer would serve Georgie the divorce papers that afternoon.

39. RADIOACTIVE RED

"Little by little the bird builds its nest."
French Proverb

Without Bessie, the house—which was crammed with furniture—felt vacant. But she couldn't leave until the movers came and took her things to her new place in a few days. Of course, an option would be to stay at her new apartment and sleep on the floor, but her body was too old for that. So she'd stay put.

Killing time, Dee roamed though the quiet rooms. Most things in the house would be left for Georgie to deal with. He could sell or keep the furniture, rugs, knickknacks, all of it. They haggled about the piano. She lost. But she really didn't care. Playing Für Elise would probably just make her sad. But then she looked at the piano. Yeah, she'd miss it. So she sat down and played.

"Are you sleeping, Bessie?" she said out loud, and then looked around the room with only herself in it, and felt dumb.

She turned the TV on, so the quiet place would feel peopled. It felt better with voices. She left it on with the volume high, and roamed around the house.

The encyclopedia in her dad's study was useless in the age of computers, but still she took down the R volume and packed it in a cardboard box with a few other books she wanted from her father's study—classics. Georgie wouldn't miss them.

Her new apartment was a total stranger, but she was excited to get acquainted. It faced the Detroit River. Sarah Palin could see Russia from her house; Dee could see Canada from her balcony. A much nicer place, she supposed. Next summer she could watch fireworks whooshing up from barges while Detroit and Windsor celebrated Canada Day and the Fourth of July.

Instead of hanging around the house all evening she decided to take a few things to the new apartment. She took the box of books out to her trunk, then went up to her bedroom and got the bird's nest Joey had found on the roof, and carefully put it on the passenger seat. She started her car, noted that the For Sale sign was still on Mr. Grouch's lawn next door. It didn't seem like he was having much luck selling. Once Georgie had spiffed up the house, Grouch's house might be worth even more. She silently wished him well too.

She sat for a moment staring at the house she'd lived in for so many years. The porch needed paint. She was leaving behind the green plastic chairs where she sat beside Bessie when the weather was kind. She'd spent the two ends of her life (childhood/youth and middle-aged/old) in that house. During the last sixteen years, all the painful memories of growing up had wrapped around her like too tight binding. If she hadn't been living in this house, Georgie's childhood pranks probably wouldn't have crossed her mind. But Georgie's presence was embedded in the walls.

Sitting in the driveway, Dee noticed several tall pokeweeds shooting up amongst the junipers—pokeweeds are poisonous. She remembered days when taking care of Bessie made her so stressed that all the hairs stood up on her arms. Dee didn't believe in the idea that everything happens for a reason. But sometimes when a bad thing happens, something good can happen in response. If there hadn't been the car accident, she would never have known the good parts of Bessie, mainly her mother's tenderness and humor.

She turned the car off and went back into the house. In the kitchen she took Bessie's favorite cup—Fiestaware radioactive red. She carried it through the house to the front door.

Bessie's black cane was propped in the corner of the entry hall. She touched it, wondered if she should take it. Stared at it. Hesitated. Georgie would probably put it in the trash. She took the cane and went out to her car. She'd put the treasures in her new apartment, spend a little time gazing south over the river at Canada, and then come back and sleep in her bed in Georgie's house.

40. BROTHERLY LOVE

"The owl is the wisest of all birds
because the more it sees, the less it talks."
Corsican Proverb

Georgie had choices. He could stay at a hotel until Dee moved out, or he could move into his house, previously known as his parents' house. He chose the latter. He had given her two weeks to move, but as he said, that didn't mean he couldn't move in. She didn't argue with him. It wouldn't be that long. No big deal.

The company that Joey sold his business to had come out to take the tarps off the roof, and when Georgie saw the name was unrelated to his ex-wife—he and Zita had made a quick unpleasant trip for a Las Vegas divorce—he hired them to do the roof. It was a big company and they were able to schedule the job that week. Later she learned from Joey, that the new company was much more expensive than he would have been.

Mostly Dee and Georgie avoided each other, although when she made coffee in the morning, she made enough for two. Habit perhaps, or generosity of spirit, or maybe just being a pushover.

On her last night before the movers came, she cooked him dinner. When he was a kid he had been a big fan of broiled chicken legs, and mashed potatoes, so that's what she made. Just like Bessie would have.

They sat in the living room with the news on TV.

"I'm sorry about Zita," she said. Of course, that was a lie, but she thought it might lead to some conversation.

"I'm not," he said, without taking his eyes off the television. "My only regret is that I didn't do it first. Who needs her? I'm glad to be done with her."

Dee knew from Zita that he had signed over their house and half their savings to her.

"Do you feel bad that she has your house?"

"Look, Dee," he actually looked at her then, "We were married a long time, any court would give her half or more of what I had. So why fight it. I gave her that house, the only good thing about it was the lap pool, and I get this house. And once it's cleaned up a bit, I'm not embarrassed to tell you, I'll make a fortune. And she won't get a dime of that. A deal's a deal. Legal. Done. She can't come back crying for more when she hears how much I make."

"Alimony?"

"She works, Makes her own money. So no alimony."

"Can I please have the piano?"

He didn't answer.

"Please, Georgie."

He took another bite of chicken. It was a really good dinner, possibly his favorite, maybe worth a piano.

"Yeah," he said. "Take it. I'll never play it."

They ate listening to the TV commentators talking for a while. Dee asked, "So what's happening with Isaiah Thomas?"

He didn't look at her, just continued staring ahead at the television, and added more food to his mouth.

Did he hear her?

"Isaiah?" she repeated, "The kid you were Big Brothering? How's that going?"

He looked at her for several seconds, and said, "He didn't like fishing."

41. HOUSING

"Little by little the bird makes his nest."
Haitian Proverb

Zita put *her* house on the market, and within two days an obese guy who loved-loved-loved that penis pool bought it with cash. Zita rented an apartment in Troy.

*

Joey had helped with Dee's apartment search, and even though the apartment on the Detroit River basically made her geographically undesirable, since his own large house was in Birmingham fifteen miles north, he never questioned her desire to live in the city.

The movers came to get Dee's full house of furniture from the basement—the red lips sofa, Sy's recliner, the Saarinen dining table and chairs, and all the boxes she hadn't opened in sixteen years. Maybe it was silly having them haul things she might just donate or throw away, but she wanted to be in her own place when she unpacked. She'd take her time figuring out which things had some meaning or utility. The movers loaded up her bed and dresser and all the things in her bedroom, and *her* piano.

Joey was with her at the house when the movers came. And of course, when they had a question, they asked him, "Sir, are we taking everything from that basement room?" or "Are we moving the washer and dryer?" And good fine man that Joe Spinelli was, he just waggled his thumb like a hitchhiker toward Dee. Then the moving men would redirect their questions to the person in charge. Her.

Later, while they watched the movers lugging Dee's past life into her new life, and stacking boxes three deep and five high in her new apartment. Joey said, "So many boxes, so little time."

Joey was retired now. His time was his own. He offered to help Dee unpack. She could probably use help, but was afraid that she'd be an emotional wreck. Every box had potential connections to her dead husband Sy (sigh). She would probably cry, and she didn't want Joey to see her cry over another man, but she didn't want to reject his help either.

Finally, she said, "I think I have to do this by myself, none of these boxes have been opened since the car accident. My parents had movers come and pack up the whole house while I was still broken. I don't even know what's in them." So many years had passed while the boxes were in Bessie's basement, years when she could have looked inside them, but she didn't. Even then, had she been afraid of how painful it would be? How it might make her hate how her life had shaped up.

He smiled, nodded. "Believe me, I understand. It's gonna be hard spousey stuff."

"Spousey stuff?"

"Yeah, you're gonna open a box and it'll be filled with Sy memories. Spousey stuff."

She laughed. "Yeah. Probably."

"After Mary died I was cleaning the basement, totally unrelated to her dying, when I found an old box of letters that we wrote each other when I was in Vietnam. It was painful, and yet good. Am I explaining that right? Does that make any sense?"

"Complete sense."

"Okay, then I'll leave you to your boxes, and how about in a few days I bring dinner over in a bag or maybe a box? Coney dogs? Pizza? I'll call you first."

And he left.

Half an hour later her door buzzer rang.

When she opened the door Joey handed her a shopping bag. Inside was a new box of tissues. He kissed her once and left.

As she worked her way through all the brown cardboard boxes, she was surprised by how few tissues she needed while unpacking. Actually, just one box got to her—a box of toy soldiers that had been her son's. She remember her tiny son on his stomach on the living room floor with all these green soldiers lined up in rows facing each other, and then, with shooting sounds coming from his young mouth, one by one they got knocked over. Her son was an adult, she couldn't say, *stop the war games, and come to dinner.* She had no say in his life. So she cried. It seemed that she only had tears for living men who were in danger.

Should she save the soldiers for her son when he eventually (hopefully) returned? Should she donate them, so some other child would find his or her calling? Actually they were Paul's. She should stick them in the back of her closet and give them to him the next time he came home. She gathered up all the tiny green men and put them in the trash.

As she continued unpacking she realized that the feelings of rediscovery wouldn't have been as good if she was still with Bessie when she unloaded boxes. She would have looked and then repacked, knowing that Bessie's things—pans, plates, silverware, towels, throw pillows—would supersede hers. Now, other than the toy soldiers, the whole unpacking business was fun. She heard herself squeal with happiness over dishes. Dishes.

42. A BIRD IN THE HOUSE

"Birds are caught with seed, men with money."
Armenian Proverb

September 16, 2008

As Dee watched TV while sitting on Sy's very comfortable recliner in her new apartment, there was constant news of the financial disaster. The bottom had fallen out of the housing market. Thousands of people around the world were going to lose their homes. David Letterman ranted about John McCain not showing up for his show. Lehman Brothers had filed for bankruptcy. The people who created the housing crash would likely go scot-free.

Except one.

Zita had called. The timing was bad for Georgie. Because of the housing crash, the Ellison house was only worth half of what he'd paid Dee. The house they grew up in wasn't ready to flip. The new roof was complete, the kitchen had been gutted, the granite counters, new cabinets, and the high-end stainless steel appliances had all been purchased, and were boxed up in the dining room—all of it bought and paid for with a very large bank loan. Instead of making a killing on the house, the house was killing him, or maybe that's sounding too dramatic.

So she called—perhaps feeling sorry for him.

"What?" he shouted into the phone, before she had a chance to say hello. "Whoever this is, I don't want any."

Understandable. She was on her cell phone and he didn't know her number. Who else was calling him that he didn't want to talk to? Debt collectors? Lawyers of women he had sexually harassed? Devastated clients screaming at him on the phone? Politicians wanting his vote? Charities wanting donations?

Then he shrieked in terror, and shouted into the phone, "Jesus! there's a bird in the house! How could a damn bird get into the house!"

He screamed again. Caught up in his fear of the bird, probably forgetting that he was still on the phone.

"Jesus! Jesus! The damn thing almost flew into my head!"

She was going to tell him to just open the front door and the bird would find it's way out, but he'd already hung up.

43. Epilogue

"People live like birds in the woods:
when the time comes, each must take flight."

Chinese Proverb

February 2009

It was snowing in Detroit. Winds were spitting tiny shards of ice at pedestrians' faces. But Dee wasn't there.

She had flown in two airplanes, one to Seattle, and one to Maui, and in a couple days she was going to float through the air on a zipline over a jungle filled with tropical flower scents, bird songs and warm breezes whispering off the ocean. She had arrived in heaven. It was as good as the dream she'd once imagined...better. Her dreams of flying were coming true.

Even from the balcony of the hotel room she could see the lushness of the island, the Pacific Ocean, the vast green lawn, the flowering trees, the swimming pool shaped like a whale, and the swaying palm trees.

The hotel management didn't want you to feed the birds, but it was too hard to resist. They perched on the railing and looked at her with hungry expectation. She'd feed them and laugh as they posed for her sketches.

She walked along the sidewalk that ran between the ocean and the resort hotels along Ka'anapali Beach on Maui. She wore a big sunhat, and clamdigger pants. Her arms were bare and just beginning to turn a little pink. She walked alone, a sketchbook and a box of colored pencils in her tote bag. Hawaii had some beautiful birds.

She had left the hotel room quietly, but the door squeaked as she closed it, waking him from a nap. So he followed her. Even from a distance you could see he was slightly shorter than her. He jogged up and took her hand. They smiled. They still had another week of vacation in Hawaii, and then they'd see what happened next.

She was open.

ACKNOWLEDGMENTS

Before *A Bird in the House* was an actual printed book, when it was still in process or finished (supposedly) with plenty of errors—typos, missed question marks, fuzzy wording, maybe even fuzzy characters or situations, kind recruits and volunteers read this novel. Friends and family are a vital part of my writing process.

When I was only a third into writing *A Bird in the House*, I reached a scary point where I was feeling vulnerable and exposed—frozen. So I asked Kim McLott, my friend since the third grade, to read what I had. The next day she called and told me to hurry up, "Get writing, and don't come out of your room until you're done." Kim wanted to know what happened next. I might never have finished without her enthusiasm.

And then there were long phone calls with Lynn Bell, helping me solve the problem of a four-year old who was smarter than she should be. And on a second read she found some hilarious typos.

Carol Winslow, brought me a pile of reference on social work and walked me through what a social worker's home visit would be like.

Ed Sharples, retired professor of literature, was as tough on me as my mother would have been, and made me reconsider several aspects of the storyline. I am grateful. Tough is GOOD.

My daughter, Sue Schoettle, said, "You write much better than the author of *Fifty Shades of Gray*," which she hated. Whew! That's a relief.

Ann Amenta said, "You can't play Fur Elise if you've never had piano lessons." So piano lessons were added.

Joy Powell's suggestions added plot depth (Dee would never fly without Joy), and her eagle eye for typos was awesome.

My writer's group (Mary Cay Dietz, Marie Miller, Marilyn Kelly, Yvette Kapan, Joann Coates, and Joy Powell) all listened to me read chapters out loud, and some even read the whole book. They gave excellent feedback, were very encouraging, and laughed in all the right places.

Barbara Aylward and Alison Rule made me feel like it was a worthy endeavor. Janette Andrews' help with the editing was outstanding.

Also, a huge thank you to Margarete Koenen, who early on said she loved the book, and also helped me create an awesome website.

And finally, thank you to my husband and final reader, John Bogner, who is always supportive and encouraging no matter what I want to do.

LYNN ARBOR

About The Author

Lynn Arbor has spent her life writing and making art. When her daughter and son were young she wrote children's books—*Grandpa's Long Red Underwear,* was published by Lothrop, Lee & Shepard Books. She contributed to a decorating column in *The Detroit News* and wrote novels. Then for twenty-five years she made her living as a graphic designer. After serious illness she left advertising and became a full-time fine art painter. For the past six years writing has occupied most of her time. She is also the author of *Intentional, a novel.* She lives in Michigan with her architect husband, John Bogner.

Website and blog: https://lynnarbor.com

LYNN ARBOR

www.ingramcontent.com/pod-product-compliance
Lightning Source LLC
Chambersburg PA
CBHW070922260626
47162CB00007B/2762